NO PLACE TO DECEIVE

(MURDER IN THE KEYS: BOOK #5)

JADEN SKYE

Books by Jaden Skye

THE CARIBBEAN MURDER SERIES
DEATH BY HONEYMOON (Book #1)
DEATH BY DIVORCE (Book #2)
DEATH BY MARRIAGE (Book #3)
DEATH BY DESIRE (Book #4)
DEATH BY DECEIT (Book #5)
DEATH BY JEALOUSY (Book #6)
DEATH BY PROPOSAL (Book #7)
DEATH BY OBSESSION (Book #8)
DEATH BY DEVOTION (Book #9)
DEATH BY BETRAYAL (Book #10)
DEATH BY REQUEST (Book #11)
DEATH BY ENGAGEMENT (Book #12)
DEATH BY SEDUCTION (Book #13)
DEATH BY TEMPTATION (Book #14)
DEATH BY INVITATION (Book #15)
DEATH BY WEDDING (Book #16)

THE TOM'S RIVER SAGA
A PERFECT STRANGER (Book #1)

MURDER IN THE KEYS
NO PLACE TO DIE (Book #1)
NO PLACE TO VANISH (Book #2)
NO PLACE FOR VENGEANCE (Book #3)
NO PLACE FOR MARRIAGE (Book #4)
NO PLACE TO DECEIVE (Book #5)

THE KILLING GAME
INVITATION TO DIE (Book #1)
INVITATION TO MADNESS (Book #2)
INVITATION TO AGONY (Book #3)

ISBN: 978-1-64029-291-8

PROLOGUE

There was something electric in the beach air today that thrilled Sam. The huge waves had finally subsided and he walked barefoot in between the flotsam and jetsam the ocean had spewed onto the craggy shore. There was nothing he loved more than the beach after a storm.

He bent over to pick up a broken shell, as he usually did. But this time something else caught his eye. It was big, solid—and it frightened him.

Sam stopped and stared. A few feet away, under a pile of driftwood, a human leg stuck out.

Sam felt as if he were in a dream.

He ran over, pulled the wood off the body, and gasped. An older man, same age as him almost, lay there. Dead. His skull appeared to be brutally crushed in. The vicious blows all over the face told a story of pain and torment.

"NO!" Sam shouted wildly to the empty sky as he leaned over the corpse, wondering what humanity had come to.

*

It seemed like no time at all before the beach was filled with cops, reporters, and photographers. Photos were being taken of the body. Yellow ribbons were being set up around the crime scene to keep people out and preserve whatever evidence hadn't been washed away.

What the hell good would it do? thought Sam. The ocean kept rolling in and out, washing all the evidence away. It probably had already. There was no chance this guy's killer could have left any footprints that hadn't been destroyed.

"Did you know the victim, buddy?" one police officer asked.

"No," Sam answered, "I didn't know the guy. Never saw him before in my life. I was just strolling the beach like I do every day."

Sam heard a cop mention that despite the injuries, it wouldn't be hard to identify the victim. In fact, someone at the scene had recognized him right away. Morton Townsend. Owned a string of medical clinics in town. He donated a lot to charity, too. In fact, his picture was in the paper regularly.

1

Very nice, thought Sam.
And what good did all that do?

CHAPTER ONE

It was already mid-summer and the heat had grown thicker, making it humid and sultry down in Key West. Dressed in thin summer clothes, Olivia and Wayne were now in their office, just finishing lunch. They'd spent the morning going over their last case, congratulating each other and taking inventory of what had happened. After lunch they planned to look at what came next. No doubt about it, they'd done wonderfully in the short time since they'd opened their private investigation firm. And it was amazing working together.

The heat was getting to Olivia, though, and she ran her hands through her long hair.

"Too hot," she breathed, taking another glass of water and drinking it quickly.

Wayne got up and pulled the cord of the overhead fan, to oblige. Unfortunately, it just whirred the warm air around. Olivia couldn't help but smile. Not only was Wayne smart and handsome, but he made her smile again and again. He always took the simplest possible way to solve whatever faced them.

"The fan is nice, but how about some central air conditioning?" Olivia quipped as she felt drops of perspiration drip down her forehead.

Wayne's eyes sparkled. "The fan is healthier for us," he replied. "What's wrong with heat when summer comes? I, for one, love it."

"And I, for one, am getting sleepy," Olivia remarked, feeling herself wilting. "And we still have a long afternoon to go." They had said that their afternoon would be devoted to getting their next case. So far, they'd easily received a great deal of publicity; many people had called for help. The problem was they could only take one case at a time. Usually there was only a brief window open after one case ended before they could take on the next.

"No worries," Wayne always remarked, "our cases are out there waiting for us. We just have to let people know that we're free when the time comes."

Olivia enjoyed Wayne's boundless optimism. So far it had worked, too. Cases had come to them naturally. But still, at that moment, when the phone rang, Olivia couldn't have possibly imagined that in the blink of an eye, their afternoon work would be done. And, before they knew it, they'd be on their way to Key Biscayne.

Not expecting anything in particular, Olivia let the phone ring a few times before she leaned over and picked it up.

"Olivia Wells? Is this Olivia Wells?" A taut young woman's voice was on the other end.

"Yes, it is," replied Olivia, alerted.

"You're the Olivia Wells of Wells and Darrington Private Investigations?" The troubled young woman needed to be sure.

"I am," Olivia spoke slowly, as she flipped on the speakerphone so Wayne could hear the call as well.

"This is Penny Townsend," the young woman breathed. "I'm sure you've heard about what happened in Key Biscayne yesterday?"

Olivia vaguely remembered a report of a murder on the news. But Wayne nodded emphatically, indicating that he knew all about it.

"Please fill me in," Olivia replied.

"My father—my father—" The young woman's voice cracked as she suddenly broke down sobbing.

"I'm so sorry." Olivia zeroed in strongly.

"Someone's killed my father and we need help," the young woman continued in a raspy tone. "My mother's going crazy, she's totally out of control. The police are on it, but it's not enough. To them it's only routine business. To us it's our whole life."

Wayne shook his head as he listened. "You've got a fine police force down there," he said loudly. But of course the woman on the phone could barely hear him.

"There's no way this should have happened," she went on. "My father was a good man, he had no enemies, believe me. We need you. My brother and I will not leave any stone unturned until we find the monster who did it. It was a horrible killing. My father suffered a lot."

"Awful," Olivia breathed as Wayne took a few steps closer, listening carefully to every word that was said.

"Thank God, I heard about you and your partner on the news during your last case," Penny continued. "Everyone down in the Keys heard about it and says you're absolutely tops."

"Thank you," Olivia responded.

"And I like the idea of having a woman detective down here with us, too. It'll be good for my mother. She's become unmoored."

4

"Does your mother want us down there on the case as well?" Olivia asked quickly.

"My mother doesn't know what she wants at this moment. You can't ask her a thing. I'm taking over for now, along with my brother Lance. Lance agrees with me about hiring you and that's enough. Are you free? Can you both come down immediately?"

Olivia took a long breath and glanced at Wayne, who strongly nodded yes.

"Fortunately, we are free right now," Olivia slowly replied.

"Thank you, thank you," Penny exclaimed. "You have no idea how much this means to me. Do you want me to book the flight down here for you? My brother will make the hotel arrangements."

"We can book the flight," said Olivia quietly.

"Charge it to my card." Penny's voice got louder. "Charge everything to my card, including whatever fees you have. I'll text you the number. But get here fast, please. My father's gone, he's dead. And who knows what's coming next? We're all alone. There's no one left to take care of us now."

CHAPTER TWO

As they boarded the plane for Key Biscayne and took their seats, Olivia moved closer to Wayne. The sky was clear and the flight was expected to land on time. Arrangements to leave had gone easily. Olivia and Wayne had packed quickly and he called to make reservations at the hotel.

"We'll get rooms down the hall from each other," Wayne said.

"Good," said Olivia lightly, although she felt a tinge of disappointment. Actually, business was all they had focused on for a while now. Neither of them had said a word about their sudden, passionate embrace as their last case was ending. The kiss had struck like lightning and had been unforgettable, at least for Olivia. It had definitely changed the equilibrium between them, she thought. Olivia was surprised that Wayne hadn't reached out again. But she knew above all that Wayne was careful and thoughtful. He wasn't someone who would allow passing impulses to take over his life. Had their embrace been only a passing impulse for him, Olivia wondered, or was there something deeper growing inside?

The plane lifted flawlessly into the cloudless sky as Wayne looked over at Olivia.

"This is magical, isn't it?" he said softly.

That was a great way of putting it, thought Olivia. "It definitely is," she agreed, hoping that Wayne was speaking about their relationship. There had been an inevitable quality about it and working together had only made their connection deeper.

"I can't get over the way cases just keep falling in our laps," Wayne added.

Olivia paused a moment. Wayne wasn't talking about his feelings for her, but about the cases they worked on, the business they were building together. In fact, right after they'd packed, they both dove into their computers, focusing on whatever information was now publicly available about the murder.

She had better listen carefully, Olivia thought. There was no point in getting pulled into something that wasn't mutual between them. Perhaps the closeness between them was only happening in her mind?

"We've certainly been fortunate about getting cases," Olivia responded lightly, pulling a bit away in her seat, closer to the plane's window.

"Agreed. Let's go over what we know now about Morton Townsend," Wayne continued. "It's good to be as prepared as possible when we arrive."

Olivia felt upset momentarily. There would have been nothing wrong with spending a moment reflecting on how good it was to be together, she thought.

"Morton owned and ran a string of health clinics," Wayne continued. "They were small, boutique operations for those who want special attention. These kinds of medical practices are becoming more common these days."

Olivia was aware of that. "I know about those operations," she commented. In fact, her own parents belonged to a practice like that. And so did her first fiancé, who had passed away after his long battle with cancer. He'd joined a small, boutique practice too late, though, after his chances were basically over. It was painful thinking of him now. Olivia looked out the plane window and rubbed her hands over her face.

"Anyway, so far, I haven't seen anything at all questionable about Morton Townsend," Wayne continued. "He was a married man with three grown children, a long-term marriage, and a fine reputation, including charitable contributions and works."

Olivia felt grateful for the research Wayne had done already. He was good at it and enjoyed it.

"Morton also had a few clinics in Nashville, Tennessee, it seems," Wayne continued. "He spent half a week there and half a week in Key Biscayne."

"Sounds like an interesting balance," Olivia remarked. "We'll have to look into both locations."

"Not immediately." Wayne raised his hand. "First we have to check in with the police in Key Biscayne and discover their overall strategy. The murder took place in Key Biscayne, so the police down there are in charge."

Olivia and Wayne usually checked in with the local police as soon as they arrived on a case and Olivia was fine with that. As a previous officer on the police force, Wayne was more sensitive to protocol than she was. Olivia was newer at this work. After her first fiancé had died, Olivia stayed alone for a while. Then she'd met Todd, had a whirlwind romance, and quickly became engaged. But to her great horror, on the very night of their beautiful engagement, Todd had been murdered.

The murder of her second fiancé, Todd, had been so shocking and devastating that it literally pulled Olivia out of the life she'd been living. She then turned into someone obsessed with finding killers. It was the only way she could make sense of what had happened to her and go forward. Olivia had become a licensed private detective, with a keen eye and a surprising talent for seeing beneath the surface and unleashing the truth.

Olivia now tossed her long, beautiful blonde hair over her shoulders and smiled. It was actually exciting to be embarking upon a new case. There was no reason to dwell upon whether or not her relationship with Wayne was going to deepen. In fact, thinking that way could become a terrible distraction. She tossed a quick look at Wayne out of the corner of her eye. He was completely absorbed on the computer, going over his research on the case.

"From the nature of the injuries described, this crime had to be personal," Wayne mumbled.

"How so?" Olivia wanted more details.

"Mort's skull was crushed badly along with the bones in his face," said Wayne. "Whoever did this was getting back at him for something, hated his guts."

"You can't jump to that conclusion yet." Olivia felt jarred. "It could have been a business deal gone bad, or someone could have been hired to take him out."

"No." Wayne showed her a picture of the body.

Olivia looked at it and shivered. Wayne was right. The killing had been intensely grisly. Many more blows than needed.

"Overkill," said Wayne.

Olivia agreed. "Why?"

"That's what we have to figure out," he replied crisply.

"It does seem like some kind of vendetta," Olivia added. "From the sound of his life, there was no reason for it, though. On the surface, everything seemed to be going smoothly. We've got a lot of digging to do."

"None of their lives goes smoothly," Wayne quipped, a flash of bitterness stinging his tone. "Scratch the surface and everyone's life is a mess. Most of the victims are tortured people, or ready to torture someone else."

"Whoa." Olivia was taken aback by Wayne's cynicism. "Not everyone's life is a mess. Not everyone is tortured! We're only seeing a slanted segment of the population, Wayne. There are people who are happy, who love each other and can be trusted."

"Really?" Wayne turned to Olivia, looking put out. "Please show those people to me."

8

Something was bothering Wayne and Olivia wasn't sure what it was. This was a side of him she hadn't seen so vividly.

"Are you saying no one can be trusted?" Olivia asked, point-blank.

"No, of course I'm not saying that," Wayne backtracked. "I'm just saying you have to be careful, very careful, before you get too involved with anyone."

Olivia thought of her relationship with Todd then. Olivia hadn't been the least bit careful about falling for him. After mourning the loss of her first fiancé for a long time, when she'd met Todd she was ready to live fully again. Their attraction happened almost instantly and she went along with it without looking back.

Todd was handsome, exciting, adventurous, daring. They'd been deliriously happy together, too. Or so she'd thought, anyway. Olivia hadn't paused to check into who he was or what his past could have told her. At that time, if anyone had told Olivia that Todd was still seeing a former girlfriend even as he became engaged to Olivia, she never would have believed it. Life had taught her otherwise, though. In fact, Wayne had been the detective on that case. Olivia originally met Wayne in Key West, as they were trying to solve Todd's murder.

"Look at what happened between you and Todd," Wayne said then, as if he were reading her mind at that moment.

"Funny, I was just thinking that," replied Olivia. "You're right, I wasn't careful at all. I went with my feelings completely."

"See what I mean?" said Wayne, softly.

"And I'm glad I did!" Olivia answered robustly. "Even though I was fooled and hurt at the end, we had real happiness together. I felt completely loved and cared for by him."

Wayne looked at Olivia, amazed. "But for how long did you feel that?" he asked.

"It doesn't matter how long, does it?" Olivia retorted. "Even a little while is wonderful."

"I don't agree." Wayne started shaking his head.

"Well, it's better than living a life of bitterness and suspicion, isn't it?" Olivia asked emphatically. "Why let one bad experience ruin everything?"

"No one is saying to live a life of bitterness and suspicion," Wayne retorted. "Just to be careful, be slow, know what you're getting into."

Olivia tossed her hair back over her shoulders again. Did anyone ever know what they were getting into? she wondered.

"I prefer the thrill of going with my feelings," she replied swiftly. "Who can fall in love being slow and careful?"

Wayne said nothing at all.

"Who can fall in love if they're always terrified of being hurt again?" she added.

Fortunately, a voice came over the loudspeaker then, interrupting their tense conversation.

"Prepare for landing," the voice proclaimed. "We've had perfect weather conditions and are arriving in Key Biscayne early."

*

Olivia and Wayne picked up their luggage and got a cab quickly. First stop, they were headed to their hotel, the Mermaid, a few miles from downtown where the police station was situated.

The cab whizzed to their destination and Olivia and Wayne looked out the windows, oddly silent during most of the drive.

"It's beautiful here," Wayne remarked slowly as they passed palm trees, blue skies, and long stretches of sand. I think you'll love the hotel I've reserved the rooms at, too."

"I'm sure I will," said Olivia as the cab drew closer to their destination and the hotel came into sight. Olivia looked the place over. It was a beautiful, medium-sized hotel, well appointed with palm trees and flowers surrounding it. A great place for a secret rendezvous, she thought.

"This is a well-known spot for bird watching," said Wayne, "and also for honeymooners."

Olivia stepped out of the cab and breathed the sweet air deeply. Why did Wayne choose a place for honeymooners? she wondered. It seemed odd to her.

"Penny suggested we come to this hotel," Wayne continued. "She said it was perfectly located, close to the family's home and also to the police station."

"I like it," Olivia decided.

"After we check in, I think the first stop for us is to the scene of the crime," Wayne said. "Then we can go meet the police."

That sounded right to Olivia, too. She wanted to stand in the place where Mort had been when he was assaulted. She wanted to see what he saw and feel who else could have been there beside him when his life had been suddenly taken away.

CHAPTER THREE

Olivia and Wayne checked into their separate rooms quickly and then went right over to the scene of the crime, the craggy beach at the edge of Key Biscayne. It was important to get here quickly, before the light of the day was gone. Actually, the time they arrived was almost the same exact moment that Mort had been found. Of course, his actual time of death was earlier; it seemed to have been right during the storm.

Standing on the shore, Olivia took in the wonderful ocean breezes. The fresh, cooler air was a relief. She and Wayne began slowly walking along the ocean's edge. Olivia always wanted to go to the scene of the crime before she heard other facts and opinions about it. She needed to experience the actual setting firsthand, see what it had to say to her directly.

"This is where the body was found." Wayne suddenly stopped, map of the crime scene in his hands. He pointed to a pile of wood that lay there, now unattended.

Olivia stopped and looked across the area. Right now there was nothing to see, just that heap of old, weather-beaten wood. Slowly, she and Wayne both walked over and stood beside it, looking around. Nothing caught their eye. The beach was empty at the moment with high dune grass swaying in the wind.

"The victim came right to this spot during the storm," Wayne commented, trying to reconstruct what had happened.

"We don't know that for sure," said Olivia. "He could have gotten here earlier, right before it."

"The time of death is presently estimated," said Wayne. "We'll find out the exact time shortly."

"Was he here alone? Was he waiting for someone?" Olivia went along with Wayne's questions.

"Important point," Wayne remarked.

"Or, was it his habit to come out on the beach and spend time here alone?" Olivia dwelled upon all possibilities.

"The victim had no weapons or protection on him when found," Wayne continued. "Seems as if he had no idea he was in danger."

"Who does?" said Olivia quietly.

"Some do," Wayne said. "Some come prepared for trouble. Some are looking for it, even."

"Funny that they left him on the beach," Olivia continued. "Whoever killed him wanted him to be found. They could just as easily have tossed him into the ocean, let his body be washed away."

"Good point." Wayne nodded. "Of course, many bodies return from the ocean to the shore, but many don't, as well."

"The killer not only wanted him to suffer, but wanted his friends and family to suffer as well," Olivia added as the winds from the ocean grew stronger. "The killer wanted everyone to see what had become of Mort. Could have been sending a message or warning to someone?"

"Killer or killers," Wayne added. "It would have been hard for one person to do this alone. Mort was a big man. Reports say he was in good health and strong."

"A gang attack?" Olivia wondered as she watched evening clouds begin to form over the sky.

"And why here on the beach?" asked Wayne. "Who even knew he would be here? Unless of course this was a random attack. Was Mort simply a target of opportunity? Or was he killed for the joy of killing? Could it be a killer seeking attention, feeling thrilled by everyone's horror and fear?"

Olivia doubted it. "Not with this level of brutality."

"The victim was found by a stray guy," Wayne added, "someone who walks on the beaches every day."

"It wouldn't hurt talking to him," Olivia commented. "Has he been questioned yet?"

"We'll find out when we talk to the police," said Wayne. "My guess is he definitely has."

"There will be a lot of people to talk to," Olivia responded, trying to sense what it would have been like to be here alone and suddenly accosted. There had to be something or someone in Mort's world that would have some clues as to what was really going on in his life.

*

Chief of Police Joe Dowl was in his office at the station waiting to meet Olivia and Wayne. Dowl was a tall, heavyset guy, with a big forehead, rough features, and a no-nonsense attitude. As soon as they arrived, he came over to greet them.

"Glad you got here so fast," Dowl said, looking at Wayne. "Your reputation precedes you. I put in a call to the guys on the force in Key West and they have nothing but the best to say about you."

"That's good to hear," replied Wayne, smiling. "And this is my partner, Olivia Wells," he introduced immediately.

"Yes, yes." Dowl picked right up on it. "Come on in, both of you. Can't ever hurt to get more eyes and hands on a case."

Olivia and Wayne followed him into his large office and sat down. The room had big windows overlooking a courtyard with benches and a few straggly trees. There was a sad feeling about the place.

"We don't get that many murders down here in Key Biscayne," Dowl started. "Usually it's theft, gang violence, assaults. Guests have property stolen from their hotels sometimes." He was defending not only his department, but the town he watched over.

"This case is a tough one," Wayne mentioned.

"Could be," Dowl agreed. "I don't know if you heard that recently we had a hardened killer let out early on parole? Everyone's jumping on that, naturally."

"No, I hadn't heard that," said Wayne, fascinated.

"Yeah, Hank Waring. There was a fuss about his being released, too. People were divided. A bunch thought he shouldn't be let free. But there's also a prisoners' rights group here in town."

"Good," Wayne echoed.

"Why was he freed?" asked Olivia sharply.

"Hank was a good inmate." Dowl scratched his face and scowled. "He did plenty of time, didn't cause trouble, and the parole board felt he was sufficiently rehabilitated to let him go."

"That seems fair," Wayne chimed in.

"Seems that way," said Dowl, "but the point is, we found him lingering on the edge of the crime scene after the victim's body was taken away."

"That's different." Wayne was quick on the uptake. "Was he there all afternoon? Or did he come when he heard the news, like everyone else?"

"We don't know that for sure." Dowl looked upset. "Right now, after this killing, there's a huge public outcry about him."

"Don't let that shake you. It's dangerous to jump to conclusions." Wayne stopped him.

"Don't I know it?" said Dowl. "Hank was taken in for questioning right away. And, although he was in the vicinity, we didn't have enough evidence to hold him. Not yet anyway. Just being in the vicinity of a crime isn't a crime in and of itself. But I wanted to let you know he was there, just in case."

"Thanks," said Wayne. "You're keeping an eye on him?"

"Naturally," said Dowl.

"How about the person who found the victim?" Olivia inquired.

"You mean Sam Rudy?" Dowl asked. "We talked to him too, naturally. There's nothing suspicious going on there. People around here know him well. He walks on the beach every day at about that hour. The guy has no connection to Mort Townsend at all."

"When will you have the exact time and cause of Mort's death?" Wayne shifted focus.

"Sooner than you think," Dowl replied. "This case is causing too much upset and we're determined to get answers fast! We do have an important fact now, though. There was no DNA evidence to suggest that the victim put up a fight."

"That's huge," said Wayne.

"Yes, it is," Dowl agreed. "It speaks to the way they got him. He was taken unaware, overpowered."

"Or it's possible he didn't put up a fight because he knew the person who came to kill him?" Wayne suggested.

"It's definitely possible," Dowl agreed. "In any case, we're glad you guys are here to join in the search."

It was good to hear that they were welcome and Olivia smiled.

"Anything else you want to know right off?" Dowl asked, still addressing his questions to Wayne only.

"I've got information about Townsend. And I'd like to keep in close touch about all our findings as the case progresses," Wayne replied.

"I wouldn't mind talking to Sam Rudy, either," Olivia suddenly joined in.

"Sam Rudy? Why?" Dowl looked disconcerted.

"Why not?" asked Olivia. "He was there at the scene and found the victim, didn't he?"

"Yeah, but Sam was not the last one to see the victim alive." Dowl didn't warm to the suggestion. "We have no idea who that was yet."

"Just a thought," Olivia remarked.

"Well, Sam's actually somewhere around right now." Dowl finally looked directly at her. "We've just finished speaking to him, as I said. I don't see the point of doing it over again."

"A few more minutes can't hurt." Wayne stood up for Olivia.

"No, I guess not." Dowl didn't look pleased. "Talk to him all you like." He turned again to Olivia. "And after you're finished, I'd say it's best to use your time interviewing Mort's family, friends, and business associates. We're talking to them too, but you guys could find a new slant. One of them has got to know something. Unless, of course, Hank got out of jail and struck again, the way a lot of folks here are saying. Some killers do that, they can't control themselves."

"Serial killers," Olivia remarked. "Has Hank killed multiple times?"

"No, just once, his ex-wife," said Dowl. "It was a long time ago. As I said, he served plenty of time."

"What would he have against Mort?" Olivia wanted answers.

Dowl shrugged and looked at her closely. "That's a good question, and you never know. Sometimes inmates are visited by outsiders and even hired to do stuff like this."

"Anything is possible," said Wayne as he threw Olivia a quick glance.

"Is there anything else?" Dowl then asked pointedly.

"Well, I wouldn't mind talking to Sam, if he's here already," Olivia remarked. Who knows, he might have noticed a detail no one else saw, she thought. That one detail could lead them to another. Often the most powerful clues came when least expected.

"Sure." Dowl got up then. "I believe Sam's still here somewhere. I'll go and get him for you."

*

Olivia was taken aback when Sam Rudy walked into the room. His overall appearance was casual, bordering on messy, but a strange intelligence surrounded him nevertheless. His piercing gray eyes shifted back and forth before landing on Olivia.

"Bad things happen everywhere," Sam suddenly grumbled before giving her a long, painful glance.

"Olivia, this is Sam Rudy," Chief of Police Dowl introduced. "You said you had a few questions for him."

Olivia nodded. "Thanks so much for your time, Sam," she said, taking a step closer to him.

"It's my pleasure," Sam answered. "After all, I'm the one who found him on the sand. I haven't been able to sleep a wink since then, either. I have no idea why it was me who found him. But there you go."

"Well, I'll leave you all alone for now," Dowl remarked, throwing Wayne a quick glance before he left the office.

"This is my partner, Wayne." Olivia introduced Wayne, who stood a few feet away. She wanted Sam to feel at ease.

"Detectives?" Sam questioned, looking back and forth at them.

"Yes, we've been brought in to help with the case," Olivia replied.

"Poor guy." Sam rubbed his big hand over his weather-beaten face. "Didn't have a chance out there. Didn't know what he was up against. He looked like a white-collar guy. Too refined, no instinct for danger."

"You knew him?" Wayne intercepted.

"No, never saw him before," said Sam. "Just heard things about him and from the looks of him lying there, they got him by surprise."

"What makes you say that?" Olivia was fascinated by everything about Sam. He was both unpretentious and powerful at the same time.

"I don't know why I'm saying that," said Sam, pulling a chair over and sitting down. "You just feel things sometimes. It looked to me like he was overpowered right where he stood. Someone took him down and crushed him right on the spot."

"I heard his eyes were closed when you found him," Wayne commented quickly. "Was there a frightened expression on his face?"

"Nah, nothing," Sam answered. "And how do I know? Sure, it's possible he could have put up a fight."

"There was no DNA evidence on him to suggest that," commented Wayne.

"You're sure you never saw him before?" Olivia questioned again. "He wasn't a beachcomber like you are, by any chance?"

At that Sam cracked an odd smile. "I never thought of myself as a beachcomber," he said, "just a guy who roams on the sand every day. There are a few of us like that, down here in the Keys."

"Was someone there regularly at that time of day? Could they have been there when Mort was killed?" Olivia jumped on it.

"Nah, not that I know of," said Sam. "Nobody else I know of goes to that beach every day. And by the time I got there, from the looks of the body, he was long gone."

"There was a storm that day, wasn't there?" Wayne remarked.

"Yeah, there was. But that doesn't stop people from coming. Beachcombers go no matter how bad the weather turns." Then Sam smiled at Olivia warmly, making her feel as though she'd found a brand new friend.

Olivia smiled back at him. "I really appreciate your help, Sam," she replied.

"You're two good folks," Sam went on. "They're lucky to have you down here, helping out. Let me know if there's anything else I can do for you."

Olivia was surprised by his offer. "Like what?" she said.

Sam shrugged. "Heck if I know. But I've been in Key Biscayne a long, long time. Give me a call if I can help with something."

"Thank you, I will," said Olivia as Sam yanked a pad out of his pocket and scrawled down his number.

After Sam left, Olivia and Wayne gathered their things to go back to the hotel.

"Let's forget about returning to the hotel right now," Wayne said suddenly. "Before we call it a day, I want to get over to the Townsend home and meet the family."

"I thought it might be better to go first thing in the morning," said Olivia. "They'll all be exhausted by now after a long day."

"Exactly." Wayne nodded. "So much the better. We'll get to see them when they're frazzled and it's harder to keep up a front that hides things from us."

CHAPTER FOUR

The Townsend home was not far from their hotel or the police station. Olivia and Wayne got into a cab and arrived there in no time. Situated at the end of a cul de sac, the home was large, modern, imposing, and set back beautifully from the street. Old willow trees lined the walkway, and a small dog ran back and forth on the side lawn, wailing. He was probably looking for his owner, calling him to come home, thought Olivia.

"The family's expecting us first thing in the morning," Wayne repeated as they walked up to the front door. "This is fine though. We'll tell them we just couldn't wait to meet them."

Wayne rang the doorbell, and they only waited a few moments before they heard the familiar voice of a young woman behind the door.

"Coming, coming," she called in a high tone. "Who is it now? Aunt May?"

The door flew open and a tall, angular, very pretty redheaded young woman stepped outside abruptly. She stopped in surprise, seeing Olivia and Wayne there.

This had to be the daughter who had hired them, thought Olivia. "Penny?" Olivia asked the moment their eyes met.

"Yes, I'm Penny." The young woman stared at Olivia. "You're Olivia and Wayne?"

"We are," Olivia responded.

"We expected you tomorrow morning." Penny seemed flustered.

"We didn't want to lose any time," responded Olivia briskly.

"Well, I guess that's a good thing," Penny remarked. "At least you care about what you're doing."

"We certainly do," Wayne joined in, wanting to be included.

"Well, come on in," Penny said then, "but the place is a mess and it's overflowing with people. We've had visitors coming nonstop. Nobody can believe what happened. Not one."

"Does your mother know we're on the case?" Wayne asked soberly.

Penny threw up her hands in despair. "I don't know what my mother knows at this point. She's on a total rampage and has been since she heard the news. She refuses to calm down for a second, just keeps going on and on about everything to the visitors."

"It'll be good for us to meet her," said Olivia.

Penny looked skeptical. "Frankly, I can't see anything at all that's good about what's happening. But come on in. I'll show you around."

Olivia and Wayne followed Penny into the large home, where a sense of chaos prevailed. The place was noisy, crammed full of visitors and disturbing to be in. As they entered the luxurious living room, Olivia saw people sitting on sofas, and standing close to each other eating snacks and drinking wine. Loud voices talked over one another, and a large dog barked in the corner.

On one paisley sofa Olivia noticed a woman in her fifties holding court. She was dressed in a long burgundy dress, with a long, handmade necklace, waving her hands and speaking loudly. That had to be Christine, Penny's mother.

"Is that woman over there your mother?" Olivia asked Penny, fascinated by the spectacle.

"Yes, she is," Penny whispered. "She's been going on and on like this all day."

"Introduce us to her," Wayne suggested.

"It'll just make her worse," Penny responded. "This isn't a good time to talk to her, really."

"It's the perfect time," Wayne countered. "We'll get to know what she's thinking and feeling and how we can be of help."

Wayne's comment seemed to calm Penny down a bit.

"I'd rather introduce you to my brother Lance first," Penny commented. "Then he can introduce you to my mother. I need a break."

"I can certainly understand." Olivia smiled at her.

"Well, at least someone can understand," said Penny. "And I can also introduce you to my mother's brother, Angie, over there. He's come, unannounced, to stay with her until things settle down. Naturally, he's beside himself."

"Naturally," said Olivia.

"My mother and her brother have always been close, but if you ask me he's making her worse. He insists that the police put surveillance on our house, is convinced my mother's also in danger and that someone is still out there, lurking around."

"Someone is still out there," Wayne agreed. "Surveillance is not a bad idea until we get a sense of what this is all about. Your mother needs to be protected."

Penny threw Wayne a disturbed glance.

"Do you live here as well?" asked Olivia.

"No, I don't. I live close by and so does my brother. We're both in our twenties and single, and we don't still live at home. Why are you asking where I live? Are you suggesting I'm in danger as well?" Penny flung a nasty glance at Olivia then.

"I'm not suggesting anything yet," Olivia replied. "How can I? I need much more information. I'm just agreeing that caution is always a good thing."

At that moment, Penny noticed a young man a few feet away. "Lance, Lance, come over here," she called to him. "Olivia and Wayne have arrived."

"Really?" he said. Looking surprised and pleased, Lance rushed over to them.

Lance was tall and well groomed, with short dark hair. He was attractive and calmer than Penny and seemed very stable, actually.

"How are you both?" Lance extended his hand to Olivia as he smiled at Wayne. "Thanks so much for getting here early."

"It's our pleasure," said Olivia. "You've got a lot on your hands."

"We all certainly do," said Lance evenly.

"Introduce them to Mom," Penny asserted.

"In a little while." Lance backed down. "I don't know if she's able to really have a calm conversation yet. Everyone here thinks that the killer who was just released from jail murdered our father. That's actually causing our mother to freak out."

"Everyone here feels that way?" asked Wayne.

"And also, I've heard the police do," Lance continued. "Everyone's horrified that that killer's not back in jail. The police had him in custody for a little while, but there wasn't enough evidence to hold him. They're keeping their eye on him, though, so that's reassuring."

This was a perfect opening to go further, thought Olivia. "There's no one else at all anyone thinks could have done this? Everyone's convinced it's the killer?"

"Everyone but Margaret," Lance remarked slowly. "She's our next door neighbor."

"Is she here?" Wayne was interested.

"Yes, she's here, but Margaret tends to be suspicious of everything. You can't put much stock in what she says," Lance replied. "We're a close family with lifelong friends. Many have gathered here. We all loved our father. The obituaries coming out in the paper have nothing but wonderful things to say about him, too."

At that, Penny spun around and walked away, her hands over her face, about to break down crying.

"Let me take you to meet our mother," Lance said then. "She's rather well known in her own way down in Key Biscayne."

"Really?" Olivia was surprised to learn that.

"Yes, Mom has a very successful line of jewelry that she designs herself. She's been in the spotlight many times, not only with Dad, but due to her own exciting life." Lance seemed proud to be talking about her.

"What's exciting about her life?" asked Olivia, interested.

"You'll see when you meet her," said Lance. "Mom's charming, lively, a big personality. She has her jewelry shows everywhere you can imagine, and reporters follow her footsteps closely."

"Sounds like she enjoys attention," Olivia remarked.

Lance suddenly smiled. "That's well put," he said. Lance stopped and really looked at Olivia. "You're awfully young to be doing work like this," he couldn't help but remark. "And you don't look anything like a detective! Nothing at all. I would have thought you were in fashion, or design."

Olivia got remarks like that routinely. Actually, it was good that no one imagined that she was a detective. She could slip in under the radar and get more information that way.

"I actually used to work in the publishing industry, doing PR," Olivia remarked.

Lance looked confused. "That's quite a shift, isn't it?"

"I like this better. And I'm good at it, too!" Olivia emphasized. "Age has nothing at all to do with it."

Lance was impressed. "Of course, I'm sure both of you will do a wonderful job," he replied. "Come on, let's go, I'll introduce you to my mother."

*

A cluster of people hovered around Christine, who half reclined on a small, plush sofa. One arm was behind her head and the other tapped on her lap repeatedly.

"I can't see how I'll ever go on again," she said, breathing heavily. "I'm nothing without him."

"Christine, Christine," a short, well-dressed woman exclaimed. "You're everything. You can do it. You're the one who made his life wonderful."

"No, I'm nothing, nothing," Christine insisted in a rising tone.

"Wrong, wrong," the woman insisted. "We all love you, we're with you. We'll help you go on."

Even in her distress Christine was magnetic. Her sharp blue eyes flashed as she looked at those gathered around her. In her mid-fifties, she was still extremely attractive too, with dark brown hair dramatically pushed back from her sculpted face. Dressed beautifully, even at this terrible time, she seemed to be holding court.

"Mom." Lance made his way through the group of people around her. "I have a couple of people here to introduce you to."

Christine barely looked over at him, just murmured something indistinguishable and, with her free hand, waved him away.

"It's important, Mom." Lance was insistent.

A large, burly man with thick salt and pepper hair who was standing beside her went over to Lance.

"Take it easy, Lance." The man pushed him back gently. "Your mother's in no mood to meet new people now."

Lance stood up taller. "They're not new people, Uncle Angie," he started.

"Give it time. Tomorrow, maybe." Angie stood firm.

"They're detectives, Angie," Lance whispered loudly enough for Olivia to hear.

Angie backed off a second. "The ones you told me about?"

"Yeah," said Lance.

"Okay, let me talk to them. Leave your mother alone. She's been breathing heavily all afternoon. The last thing we need is for her to have a heart attack and lose her too."

"She's not going to have a heart attack." Lance kept calm. "She breathes heavily like that all the time. I think Mom would want to meet them."

"But she doesn't right now." Angie wouldn't have it. "In fact, she keeps thinking your father is about to walk in the door at any moment. She keeps telling me this is all a crazy dream. Then when she realizes it's not a dream, that he's really gone, she's in complete despair."

Olivia looked over at Christine carefully. She didn't seem exactly to be in despair, perhaps a state of semi-hysteria. It was understandable, naturally.

"I'll talk to the detectives," Angie repeated, "and they can speak to your mother when she quiets down."

"Okay, come here," Lance relented. There was nothing else he could do.

Angie walked directly behind Lance then and approached Olivia and Wayne bluntly.

"Heard about you guys," Angie started, "even though I wasn't consulted about whether or not to bring you on board. If I'd thought about it carefully, I don't know what I would have said."

"We weren't expecting you to move in with Mom." Lance grew irritated. "We called for the detectives before you arrived."

"It's okay, I'm not saying you shouldn't have done it. Just that I wasn't consulted about it," Angie repeated, put out.

Wayne broke into the conversation then, trying to establish rapport with Angie. "We're very glad to meet you, Angie. It seems you're an important person in the family."

Wayne's comment pleased Angie. "I've been close to my sister my whole life long," he blurted out. "And I'll be damned if I'm going to let anyone or anything hurt her now."

"This has to have come as a great shock to you," Olivia commented.

Angie turned to Olivia heavily. "That's an understatement if I ever heard one. It's a great shock to everyone, not only the family, but the entire community. There's no way to prepare for something like this."

"No, there isn't," Olivia agreed.

"Everyone's thinking it's that crazy killer they lot out of jail early. He's still on the loose, too. They haven't taken him in. For all we know, he could strike again at any second. He'd better not come anywhere near here, or he's dead on my doorstep."

"Does anyone at all have a different take on who could have killed Mort?" Wayne asked carefully.

Angie's eyebrows lifted nervously. "What do you mean? Is there anyone who suspects someone else?"

"We have to ask questions like this," Wayne assured him. "That's what we're here for. We can't leave any stone unturned."

"No one that I know," Angie answered gruffly, "except maybe Margaret, the crazy neighbor next door. But she looks at everyone with a suspicious eye. If she gets the wrong change at the store, she'll gossip about the woman at the counter, believe she did it purposely, to short-change her. You can't put stock in anything she says at all."

"I heard Margaret's here now," Olivia remarked.

"Who cares?" Angie said. "The last thing we need is having her put crazy ideas in Christine's head. Look, we're a good family, we take care of each other, hang together. I believe Mort was a target of opportunity for that deranged killer. And basically, even though it's too early to say publicly, the police agree with me. Once these killers get loose everyone knows they can't wait to get a taste of blood again."

Olivia remained silent, wondering how Angie knew that.

"Some do, some don't," Wayne declared. "It's dangerous to generalize."

Angie scratched his face. "We can talk more later, if you want. This isn't a good time for me. I've got a house full of people here, all going crazy. Just focus on nabbing that killer." Then Angie nodded his head, turned, and departed.

"From the looks of it up front," Wayne remarked after Angie left, "the family seems to be normal enough. They're all here, supporting each other. There's no glaring reason, at the moment, to suspect any of them."

"Not yet," Olivia murmured softly. "And if there is a reason, it's certainly not glaring. They look like a close enough family on the surface at least."

"And there's no evidence that I've heard about to hold that killer, either," Wayne mused. "Just being in the vicinity of a crime and having a record doesn't implicate anyone. I can see why he could look suspicious, though."

"I don't see that," Olivia suddenly countered. "I don't believe this was a crime of opportunity. Something else is going on here. The manner of death and wounds were too personal and vicious for that."

CHAPTER FIVE

"Let's have dinner up in your room," Wayne said when they were back in the cab on their way to the hotel. "It's been a long day."

"Good idea." Olivia felt the same way, tired, hungry, and eager to unwind together and go over what they had so far. She also badly wanted to put her head on Wayne's shoulder for a while and be close. They hadn't had any physical contact for such a long while, hadn't even held hands. Olivia missed it.

Olivia and Wayne went into her room, ordered salad, pasta, and red wine, and opened the windows to let the refreshing evening breeze drift in.

"I'd say we have our hands full with this case," Wayne said as he sat down on the couch, running his hands through his hair while he waited for the food to arrive. "It's probably best to divide the tasks up like we always do. I'll go and check out Mort's clinics and business associates. The police are doing a forensic review of the money, naturally. It's very important to see if he was up to anything illegal, of course."

Olivia sat down beside him. "Good plan," she agreed. "And I'll speak to Mort's family and friends in depth." This was the way they often proceeded and it had served them well so far. "Are you hungry?" she asked then. They didn't have much material to go over yet and Olivia wanted to turn both the conversation and the evening in a more personal direction.

"I'm actually starving." Wayne smiled at her. "How about you?"

"Famished," Olivia replied, moving closer to him on the couch.

"Sorry I didn't realize that." Wayne paused a moment. "I should have bought you something to eat as the day went along. What was I thinking? I can get so caught up. I don't mean to, though."

Olivia smiled. Wayne had moments of such sweetness and concern. But then suddenly he'd switch and be all business.

"Well, at least we can enjoy the evening now," Olivia offered. "Dinner and wine will be perfect. We can also put on some soft music, too."

Wayne smiled, closing his eyes momentarily.

Olivia reached over then and put her hand on his. He looked down at it a moment and squeezed her hand tight.

Olivia looked up into his eyes. "It feels so good to be here close to you," she said.

Wayne put his arm around her shoulder, pulled her to him, and gave her a light kiss and embrace. It felt right and natural to be together this way. Olivia wanted more, but then everything stopped suddenly.

"Where's the food?" Wayne asked.

"This is better than food," Olivia murmured.

But Wayne stood up from the couch abruptly and walked to the door, looking at his watch. "We've been waiting longer than usual, haven't we?" he remarked.

Disheartened, Olivia wondered what was going on with him. He seemed alarmed by the prospect of getting closer. What could possibly be next between them? Maybe nothing, she suddenly thought.

Olivia got up from the couch and walked over to where he was standing. "What's wrong, Wayne?" she asked directly.

"Wrong?" Wayne seemed discomfited.

"It seems there's something's in the way between us," Olivia went on softly. "We get close and then it disappears."

"It doesn't disappear," he said, looking straight ahead. "It just doesn't go further."

Olivia needed more than that. "Why doesn't it go further?" she asked.

Wayne turned and looked at her directly. "You know that my ex was killed in a car accident," he suddenly said, mournfully. "I told you how hard it was for me for a long time after."

"Yes." Olivia recalled Wayne telling her that. She had been surprised and saddened by the story.

"Later on I dated several people," Wayne continued, "and nothing worked out. Not one relationship lasted. It couldn't."

"Why couldn't it?" Olivia felt dismayed.

"I'm not sure," said Wayne, "but I know what we have here and I don't want to ruin it. We work fabulously together. We're great partners and I love that."

"I love it too," said Olivia.

"It would be a mistake to threaten what we actually have," Wayne repeated sadly, as finally, someone knocked on the door.

"Just leave the food outside," Olivia called out.

"Let's take the food in now." Wayne looked troubled.

"In a minute," said Olivia. "First tell me why no other relationship could ever work out for you."

"I don't know, maybe it could, I'm not sure." Wayne seemed nervous. "I wish it could, but I don't trust it."

"You don't trust women?" Olivia asked, disconsolately.

"I don't trust myself," Wayne answered slowly. "I don't trust the whole process and I just couldn't stand going through another breakup. Especially with you! Especially!"

Olivia appreciated his honesty deeply. She suddenly wanted to throw her arms around him and hold him close.

"I lost two fiancés myself," Olivia said softly. "One to cancer and the other to murder and infidelity. But I'm still willing to try."

"You're a brave woman, Olivia," Wayne said. "I saw that about you immediately. You're beautiful, too. You move me, impress me. You inspire me totally."

"So hold me again," Olivia whispered.

Wayne looked at her sadly. "Let's have dinner now, please," he pleaded as he went to the door to bring in the food.

Olivia took a step back as she wondered if something else was wrong. Did Wayne have trouble getting close to women in general? Was the death of his ex was just an excuse? Maybe he was right and they should just leave well enough alone. As it was, their relationship worked perfectly. Wayne was a wonderful support and partner in every way. But something else tugged deep inside of Olivia's heart. And it was hard to shut it off and put it away.

Olivia couldn't help but think of Todd and how joyous it had been to be with him. There were been no hold-backs between them. Both went with the moment, jumped into their feelings, let it take them wherever it did as if they were surfing waves in the ocean. When she and Todd had been together, a sense of oneness had pervaded Olivia's life. True, it had ended horribly and abruptly, but that didn't take away from the happiness she'd known. She wanted it back. Life without Todd lacked something deeply important.

Olivia looked at Wayne again now. She could see herself getting there with him, too. Wayne was different from Todd, but wonderful in his way. Of course, the feelings between them had to be mutual, and clearly, they weren't right now. Olivia felt she had to accept the good they had, and leave the rest alone. It didn't make sense to push for things to be different. Wayne was right, she'd mess up what they did have.

Wayne opened the door then, rolled in the dinner cart, and took the lids off the dishes. Olivia went over to the TV and turned it on. It would be a casual dinner.

"The food looks wonderful," Wayne said, more cheerful then.

"Great, let's have some," Olivia replied, returning to their usual way of being together and letting the moments of intimacy melt away.

Suddenly the TV station flashed a Breaking News alert.

"Breaking news!" The reporter's voice grew louder. "Hank Waring, formerly in jail for murder, has suddenly left town!"

"Oh boy!" Wayne called out.

"The former inmate, who was questioned regarding the Townsend murder, has apparently hightailed it out of town! Not only is that a parole violation, but he had given guarantees he would remain close by. Police in neighboring towns are mobilized, searching for him right now."

A photo of Hank Warning, dressed as an inmate, flashed on the screen.

"If you've seen him anywhere at all, please call the number on the bottom of the screen!" the reporter insisted. "And be careful! It's likely that he's armed and dangerous."

"Oh God," said Olivia, "this doesn't look good. The case may have ended before it began."

"Not really." Wayne refused to jump on the bandwagon. "Hank could have panicked and felt the cops were closing in."

"Nobody was closing in," Olivia objected. "He was questioned and released."

"But it's understandable that he felt like a sitting duck just waiting for them to get him," Wayne insisted.

As Wayne was involved working with restorative justice, Olivia noticed that initially he always took the side of anyone who'd been imprisoned. He wouldn't let anyone jump to conclusions.

"The police do it all the time," Wayne said again now. "It's convenient to grab an ex-inmate, without sufficient evidence, and pin suspicion on them. It's a mistake though, a big mistake. It takes the focus off plenty of others who are drifting in the shadows, getting away with everything."

The reporter's voice got louder with a sense of urgency in it. "As we said, please keep your eyes open for Hank Waring. There's a handsome reward for anyone who spots him. Mort Townsend's family demands justice for his horrible death."

*

After dinner, Wayne returned to his room down the hallway. The plan was that Olivia would return to the Townsend home in the morning to speak to Penny and Lance in depth. And, if possible, Mort's wife, Christine. Wayne would go to Mort's clinics and familiarize himself with those who worked there and the work Mort was involved in.

When Wayne left, Olivia walked out onto the small balcony in the room, overlooking the hotel gardens. It was a beautiful night with a crescent moon in the sky. She would have loved to walk down there in the gardens, arm in arm with someone she cared for. It would have been a resting place away from the endless anxiety that surrounded each case of murder. Without that, the work could feel relentless. There were no breaks from the horror and fear everyone seemed to be surrounded in.

CHAPTER SIX

The next morning, Olivia decided to have breakfast in her room alone before going off to the Townsends' home. Usually she and Wayne connected first thing in the morning and had breakfast together. After that they'd embark upon the day. But this morning Olivia didn't want to. Instead, she got up early and called for some scrambled eggs, coffee, and toast. Then she dressed in a lovely, light blue, printed silk dress, put on open sandals, brushed her hair a long time, and looked at herself in the mirror. If Wayne wasn't interested in her, someone else surely would be. She was young and people said she was beautiful. But more than all of that, she had so much to give the right person.

Breakfast came quickly, and as soon as she'd eaten, Olivia left the hotel to go speak to Penny and Lance. Hopefully, she would also be able to get some time with Christine. But who knew if Christine would be up for it yet?

Fortunately, when Olivia arrived at the Townsend home, the door was half open. Even though it was early, their day had begun. Olivia stood outside and rang the bell anyway. After a few minutes, Penny arrived in the doorway, dressed in a short skirt and T-shirt.

"Oh my God, you're so early," said Penny, frazzled.

"I can come back in a little while if that's better," offered Olivia.

"No, not at all. The earlier the better," Penny exclaimed. "Come in, come in."

Olivia followed her into the house, which still seemed messy and in disarray.

"Everyone's freaking out about the news that the killer left town!" Penny uttered. "Tons of people have been calling us about it."

"Big mistake," agreed Olivia. "He shouldn't have done that."

"Big mistake? That's putting it mildly!" Penny stared at her. "It makes him look guilty as hell, doesn't it?"

"Looks like it," Olivia agreed, "but people run away for all kinds of reasons."

"My mother's positive he did it," Penny breathed. "She said she's glad he ran away and made his guilt so public."

"We still have to keep investigating," Olivia insisted. "Until we're sure, we can't stop."

"Of course," Penny agreed. "You seem so smart, how come?"

Olivia smiled. "I'm just good at this," she answered lightly. "I'm not so smart about everything, though."

Penny liked that. "Come on into the kitchen. Lance is there having coffee. Our older brother, Thomas, is out of the country."

Olivia was startled; she didn't realize they had an older brother. "What's Thomas doing there?"

Penny shrugged aimlessly. "Who knows? Thomas barely stays in touch with us anymore. It's one thing after another."

"That's rough," said Olivia as they got into the big, white-tiled kitchen that had a beautiful round table in the corner, where Lance sat drinking coffee, the paper spread out before him.

"It's not rough on us anymore," said Penny. "We're used to it. After college Thomas went to live in Europe and by now, we hear from him occasionally at best. He lives in one country and then another. Seems he has all kinds of odd friends over there that he doesn't want us to know anything about."

"Does Thomas know about what happened to your father?" asked Olivia.

"My mom has been trying to reach him frantically," said Penny. "So far I don't know if she's been able to. She's the only one who manages to keep even slightly in touch with him."

Lance stood up then. "Talking about Thomas?" he asked as Penny and Olivia came over to the table where he had been seated. "I'd say he's barely a family member by now."

"That happens in many families," Olivia said, thinking of her own twin sister, Mauve. Olivia had barely seen her for the past year. "People drift off in different directions."

"Please sit down, won't you?" Lance said, sitting again.

Olivia sat down.

"Thankfully, Lance and I are very close," said Penny as she sat down beside Olivia. "And I have a best friend, Andrea, who's like a sister to me."

"Good," said Olivia. "It's amazing how friends can turn into family."

Lance grimaced. "Family is family," he said, "and friends are friends."

"Lance is very literal," said Penny. "He likes to call something exactly what it is and take things as they come. Lance is going to be the best possible lawyer, ever."

Olivia was impressed. He did seem as if he'd make a wonderful lawyer, the way he attended to details and facts.

"How are you doing, Lance?" Olivia turned toward him, taken by his calm demeanor. How could he be so unruffled, she wondered, so soon after his father had been murdered? Had that fact even hit Lance yet?

"I am doing all right," Lance replied. "What good would it do if I went crazy now? My job is to keep the family together and learn as much as I can about the crime."

Lance would also be a fantastic detective, Olivia thought. "And what have you learned so far? Who do you think could be involved?" Olivia asked quickly.

"No one in the family, naturally," Lance replied immediately. "Despite Thomas, we have a happy family and we had a great dad. My father was someone you could count on totally."

"He traveled a lot for work though, didn't he?" Olivia asked.

"He was in Nashville half a week and half a week here." Lance smiled. "He had clinics there. It was natural, we were all used to it. And it was fun in a way. When he came home, he always brought us gifts."

"Really? What kind of gifts?" Olivia was surprised.

"Gifts, all kinds." Lance smiled. "Whatever we were into, sports for me, books and recordings for Penny, and usually jewelry for Mom."

Penny stood up then and ran to the sink to pour herself a glass of water.

"Did it bother you that your dad was gone half the week, Penny?" Olivia asked.

"No, it didn't. Nothing about him bothered me," Penny insisted, drinking the water quickly before she returned. "I knew he cared about me totally and that he still does."

"Still does?" Lance looked at Penny oddly.

"He still does," Penny insisted. "I see my dad in my dreams every night now and I know that he stills cares for me."

Lance shook his head slowly. "Sometimes Penny can be a bit like Mom," he murmured.

"In what way?" Olivia was fascinated.

"Dramatic," Lance murmured. "As you know, our mother is a very dramatic individual. Penny's really not like that, but once in a while, it breaks through. She imagines things."

"There's nothing dramatic about having dreams about someone you loved, who died," Penny insisted.

"Of course not," Lance agreed, "but to say he still loves you? It's just a way of keeping him alive in your mind."

Penny took a deep breath. "You can't argue with Lance. There's no point to it. If he doesn't believe something, he refuses to even consider the matter. But I talk it over with my friend Andrea, and thankfully, she understands everything I say."

"How about your mother?" asked Olivia.

"What about her?" Penny withdrew for a moment.

"Can you discuss these kinds of things with her as well?"

"Excuse me," Lance interrupted then, "but what has this got to do with anything?"

"I'd like to know more about your family dynamics," Olivia answered plainly. "It can help me understand your father and what might have happened to him."

"As I said, we have a fine family," Lance repeated emphatically. "Mom can be a bit hard to handle, especially when something goes wrong. But my parents had a wonderful marriage, if that's what you're wondering about. He was always good to her and she was always good to him. Everyone will say so."

Olivia looked at Penny, who nodded intensely. "My father was always good to everybody," Penny exclaimed fervently.

"It's nice to hear that," Olivia responded. "And it's pretty rare to hear about a long, wonderful marriage these days."

"Well, my father was a rare man," Lance insisted. "Frankly, as I see it, his murder was due to the fact that he became a target of opportunity for that deranged killer. There's no other possible explanation for it."

There were always other possible explanations, thought Olivia. But it seemed that it was impossible for either Penny or Lance to even imagine that anyone might have willfully harmed their dad.

"Can I speak to your mother now?" Olivia asked then.

"Yes, you can, but not now," Lance said. "We had to give her medication to sleep last night. She hasn't woken yet. It's best to let her rest as long as she can. This is having a terrible effect on her."

"Of course," Olivia agreed, standing up then.

"I'll contact you as soon as our mom is able to talk to you," Lance added.

Penny stood up, too.

"There are other people you can talk to though," Lance offered, taking a piece of paper from his pocket. "I've prepared a list of neighbors and friends and their phone numbers for you. They'll all tell you the same thing, though. My dad was a good man, a wonderful husband and perfect father."

Olivia took the paper gratefully. "Thanks for this," she said, turning to go to the door.

"Stay in touch with us," Penny chimed in. "Let us know what you're finding."

"Of course," said Olivia. "I'll stay in touch closely. Things change moment to moment in a case like this. New information always becomes available. If you hear anything at all, contact me as well."

"I definitely will," said Penny, her face looking drawn and agitated suddenly.

CHAPTER SEVEN

Wayne called Olivia's room first thing in the morning, as usual, and was startled when she didn't pick up. He immediately ran down the hallway and knocked on the door. No answer. Was something wrong, or had she just gone out on her own, without telling him?

Rather than calling downstairs to the lobby to check if they'd seen her, Wayne decided to send her a quick text.

Is something wrong? Where are you? he texted, uneasily.

Thankfully, in a few minutes, Olivia replied.

Wanted to get an early start at the Townsend home, she answered. *All good.*

Of course all was not good and Wayne realized it. Olivia was probably reacting to what happened between them last night, he thought. All the more proof of what he feared. If even a small discussion about their relationship had this kind of effect, imagine what would happen if they had really become an item. Wayne took a deep breath. This upset between them had to be nipped in the bud before it went further and created a real mess.

All is not good, he decided to text Olivia back. *You're mad at me because of last night and so you just took off without telling me or having breakfast together. It would have been nice if you'd let me know in advance you were going to do that.*

Wayne waited a few moments then and no answer came. This was exactly what he'd predicted. For all he knew, things were now over. But to his surprise, suddenly, a text popped up.

You're right. I'm so sorry, Olivia texted back. *I behaved foolishly. What was I thinking? That shouldn't have happened. It won't again. I actually didn't even realize it fully. And now I also see you're right—we have to keep things on a professional basis only.*

Wayne was actually startled by Olivia's response. It was the last thing he'd expected. She was so clear and honest with him, even took the blame. That was totally unusual. Not only did he greatly appreciate it, but it made him wonder if he'd been mistaken.

Thanks for that, he texted back. *I really appreciate your honesty.*

I really appreciate you, too, said Olivia. *Let's just put all the rest on the back burner and go on with our work.*

Once again Wayne was both relieved and yet oddly disappointed.

Great, he said. *I'm going to Mort's clinic now.*

Good, texted Olivia. *I've just finished at the Townsend home for the morning. Lance gave me a list of friends and neighbors to call. We'll fill each other in later on.*

*

Wayne took a cab downtown to Mort's main clinic, relieved that Olivia wasn't with him right now. He hadn't seen their altercation coming and needed a little time alone to get back in balance. Wayne had been through the exact same thing with his other relationships. This was always how it started. The women began to pull away without warning. For the first time now, though, Wayne stopped and wondered what he might have had to do with it. The thought itself was startling to him. But the way Olivia responded was definitely different from the others. It caused him to think.

Wayne arrived at Mort's main clinic and was ushered right into the office of Guy Harpin, the top administrator. Guy was a tall, stately man in his early fifties, well dressed and gracious. He actually seemed pleased to see Wayne. Of course, all this had to be extremely unnerving for him, Wayne realized.

"So glad to see you, come in." Guy extended his hand warmly to Wayne.

"Good to see you as well," Wayne replied, feeling calmer now and back on track. He walked into Guy's office, which was large and beautifully decorated with wood-framed photos of rivers and waterfalls over the wall.

"This is quite an operation you're running," Wayne started.

Guy looked around the room quickly. "It's all Mort's," he said quickly. "The guy did a fantastic job, getting these clinics up and going. He did a wonderful job running them and keeping everyone who worked for him well cared for and happy. Not only here but also in Nashville. Mort duplicated this model there as well. I'm actually in charge of the entire operation."

That was quite a testimony and Wayne took it in deeply. "Sounds like you really respected and cared for Mort," Wayne remarked.

"That's putting it mildly," said Guy. "I knew Mort for years, worked with him almost since the place opened. After the first clinic did so well, he decided to open others. We hired the best professional help to care for patients and made sure cutting-edge treatments were available, too. Almost no waiting time for anything."

"Too good to be true," Wayne murmured.

"It's a good model for medical care," said Guy, "only a bit pricey."

"No scandals here, or anything like that?" Wayne slipped in. "Any people upset about not getting what they needed? No irate customers?"

Guy looked at Wayne oddly. "Definitely not," he said. "Did someone say something like that to you?"

"No, no," Wayne assured him. "I'm just exploring any possibilities that could have led to Mort's murder."

"I see." Guy became quieter then.

"You worked with Mort closely," Wayne repeated. "You knew him well and you also know all the people who worked for him."

"That's right," said Guy, closing down a bit. Wayne's questions seemed to be hitting too close to him.

"Is there anything that happened here that you think could be connected to Mort's death?" Wayne felt sorry he had to be so blunt, but he had no choice about it.

"Don't think I haven't been thinking about that," Guy answered. "I've been wracking my brains, actually."

"And?" asked Wayne.

"Mostly I've been thinking about Mort," Guy went on. "I can't believe he's gone. It won't be the same without him. He didn't deserve this kind of death."

"Did Mort have any idea at all he was in danger?" Wayne probed.

"How could he?" Guy seemed startled by that question. "He wasn't in danger. His life was going just fine. There was nothing at all unusual happening. He was on top of everything."

"Or so it seemed anyway," said Wayne.

"No, it was so!" Guy insisted. "We all think it's the felon who was released from jail who killed him. Mort was in the wrong place at the wrong time. The bastard must have been hungry to kill again. I heard that someone just spotted Hank, though, two towns over. They're closing in on him as we speak."

"Wait a minute." Wayne felt suddenly chilled. "When did you hear that?"

"Just before you arrived." Wayne wet his lips slowly. "The case will be closed in no time at all."

"Could be, but it also might not. It's easy to blame the convict. That way we avoid looking deeper at what might have been going on right here, under everyone's nose."

Guy seemed startled. "Nothing was going on, I told you," he replied, taken aback.

"Think carefully, Guy." Wayne needed more information. "There had to be friction somewhere here. No organization is totally free of it."

"Of course." Wayne backed down. "We have our share of normal friction, but it didn't amount to anything. People disagree, naturally. Some are even jealous of each other. So what?"

"That's what I'm talking about. What are they jealous of? Tell me." Wayne jumped on it.

Guy seemed at a loss.

"Think harder, Guy." Wayne started pushing him. It definitely seemed that he was covering something up.

"Well, I guess there was some tension at times caused by Mort's wife, Christine," Guy said, relenting.

"Really?" This was the first time there'd been a crack in the appearance of perfection that everyone was trying so hard to create.

"There was definitely someone in the office who was jealous of Christine," Guy continued. "Whenever Christine came to visit, this person got especially snippy. And she'd start gossiping about Christine like crazy, after Christine left."

"Now we're getting somewhere," said Wayne. "Who?"

"I warned Mort about it a few times," Wayne went on, ignoring the question. "In fact, I told him that Christine was too flamboyant; she talked too loud and flashed her jewelry. It got on people's nerves. Mort should get her to pipe down."

Wayne was intrigued. "Did he?"

"He couldn't." Guy's voice lowered. "Mort said his wife was her own person and he couldn't change her, had to let her behave as she did. But let's face it, how many guys can change their wives or get them to listen to what they say?"

Despite himself, Wayne cracked a smile. That was true and he realized it. "What about the finances here?" Wayne decided to try another track. He knew there was an official financial investigation going on, but Guy could have access to information that was hard to get.

"The finances are fine," said Guy, "everything's in order. A certain amount of Mort's funds in his personal account here are unaccounted for each year. However, taxes are fully paid on them. Nothing at all illegal going on."

Unaccounted-for money was a red flag to Wayne, though. "Why was the money unaccounted for? Where did it go? Was Mort feeding money to someone?"

Guy looked away. "I have no idea what Mort did with his personal funds. I never would even ask him something like that. Mort was private about lots of things, especially his personal life. He made sure his kids kept things close to the vest, too. He monitored their social media and made sure they never divulged personal information to strangers. So these were his personal funds. How could I ask about them?"

"But we have to know where the money went," Wayne insisted. "This is the most important piece of information I have so far. Is it possible someone was blackmailing Mort?"

Guy made a sour face. "That's just ridiculous," he responded. "Don't make more of it than it is. Mort was a generous guy, always giving bonuses and gifts whenever he could."

"Who is the one here who was jealous of his wife?" Wayne returned to his unanswered question. "Did Mort give that person as much as others?"

"Mort was fair to all," Guy repeated, standing up now to indicate the interview was about to be over.

But Wayne wasn't going anywhere yet. It was clear that Guy was withholding information and Wayne was determined to find out what it was.

"Who was the person that was jealous, Guy? Why aren't you telling me? It's important. You can't withhold information like this."

Guy rubbed his hand on his arm slowly. "It's a young woman who works here named Andrea. She's actually Mort's daughter, Penny's, best friend."

"Strange that her friend would work here," Wayne commented.

"Not at all. Andrea needed a job and of course Penny pushed for her to get it," said Guy. "Andrea's a medical assistant and does a fine job, too. There's nothing at all wrong."

"Is Andrea at work here today?"

"No, of course not," said Guy. "Several people haven't been able to come in since Mort was killed. They're traumatized and we're offering a few days off until things settle down."

"What's Andrea so jealous of?" Wayne continued.

"I can't answer that, I don't really know." Guy now seemed irritated. "People say she's just a jealous person, always watching what others are getting and how they behave."

"Give me her contact information immediately," said Wayne.

Guy hesitated. "She won't talk to you much."

"It's okay, I have a terrific female partner who's very good with young women," Wayne answered quickly.

Guy reluctantly handed Wayne Andrea's contact information.

"I appreciate it," said Wayne.

"Good for you that you have a terrific female partner to help with the rough spots." Guy smiled, obviously pleased that the interview was done.

*

Wayne left the clinic stirred up. Things were too picture perfect to suit him right now. So far it definitely pointed to a random killer, but at least he had Andrea's contact information. It would work better to have Olivia talk to her. Wayne felt a little uneasy about contacting Olivia now, but shrugged the feeling off immediately. They'd gotten things back on track and he wasn't going to dwell on it. He'd just act like nothing had happened and move right along.

Instead of waiting to see her in person, Wayne put in a quick call. Fortunately, Olivia picked up immediately.

"I just got finished talking to the head administrator at Mort's clinic," Wayne said.

Olivia didn't miss a beat. "How did it go?"

"Okay, not great," Wayne replied. "I'll tell you more when I see you, but for now it's important that you contact Penny's best friend, Andrea, and interview her right away. She's the only possible lead we have so far. Andrea works at Mort's clinic and Guy said she was jealous of Mort's wife."

Olivia became silent for a moment. "That's odd," she said.

"Yes, it is a bit," Wayne agreed, relieved that he and Olivia were back on course. "Andrea's home from work today and I have her phone number. Why not give her a call and go over and see her as soon as you can?"

"Sounds good," Olivia agreed. "Is there something I'm looking for in particular?"

"Focus on Christine," Wayne suggested. "She's the one that Andrea's upset with. At least it's a good way to begin."

"I'm on it," Olivia replied. "I'll speak to her now."

CHAPTER EIGHT

Not only was Andrea in when Olivia called, but she agreed to the interview immediately.

"I live a few blocks away from Penny," Andrea said. "Come right over. I need to talk, anyhow."

Olivia left the hotel quickly, grabbed a cab, and was at Andrea's garden apartment in less than fifteen minutes. When she got to the door, to Olivia's surprise, it was open, waiting for her.

"Come in," Andrea called as Olivia paused and knocked.

Olivia entered a spacious hallway that led to a living room off to the right. When Olivia walked in, she saw Andrea sitting, curled up on a chair in the corner. She was dressed in dark cotton slacks and a black shirt. Her long, rather stringy dark hair was uncombed and, sitting there in the chair, she looked uneasy. To Olivia's surprise, Andrea did not get up to greet her.

Olivia looked around. The rest of the room was haphazard and messy, with papers and magazines scattered here and there.

"Hello, Andrea, I'm Olivia," she said as she walked over to where Andrea was sitting.

"I heard about you from Penny. You're just a little bit older than me, not much," Andrea commented as she looked Olivia over.

"That's true," said Olivia lightly, not going further with it.

"I've been Penny's best friend since high school," Andrea announced proudly. "We've been inseparable since the day we met."

"So great to have a best friend like that," Olivia murmured.

"Penny's more like a sister," Andrea corrected herself.

"Definitely," agreed Olivia. It was good that they were close in age and Andrea would feel that Olivia could understand her.

"Do you have a sister?" Andrea asked.

"I do," Olivia replied, not wanting to get into it. She had no intention of telling Andrea that she actually had a twin sister, Mauve, and that the two of them had always been distant. In fact, Olivia had always longed for a sister to be close to.

Andrea tucked her chin in further and curled her arms tighter around herself. "Most people have either a sister or brother or someone," she said bitterly.

Olivia was surprised by her bitterness. "Are you an only child?"

"You could put it that way," Andrea mumbled. "I never met my real parents. I was raised by foster parents, who never adopted me. They kept me after I aged out, though. I'm grateful for that, at least."

"They raised you here in Key Biscayne?" Olivia found Andrea interesting.

"No. They moved here when I was in high school, which was when I met Penny. We were both on the debate team."

"That's interesting," said Olivia.

"Penny and I always saw eye to eye and that's never changed," Andrea declared, carefully positioning herself.

"That's fortunate," murmured Olivia. "Friends can become closer than family."

Andrea perked up at that comment. "You can say that again!" she burst out. "A good friend is family, no doubt about it."

"How's Penny doing?" asked Olivia.

"How can she be doing? Her father's dead." Andrea became mournful. "Part of her knows it and part is still in shock. When it all sinks in and Penny really realizes that he's gone, she'll probably fall apart totally. I'll be around, though, to pick up the pieces."

"How about you?" Olivia eased into the question slowly. Actually, Andrea seemed extremely disturbed by the murder, more than Penny had, actually.

"I'm not doing so great, to be honest," Andrea answered quickly. "How can I be? I feel even worse about this than Penny."

"How come?" Olivia was fascinated.

"Penny blocks things out." Andrea rocked back and forth on her chair. "And she leans on Lance, her brother. Penny's always had someone to lean on, either Lance or her father or mother! Penny's had it all, including plenty of money in her pockets. She's not used to being abandoned."

"Unlike you," Olivia commented softly.

"That's right," said Andrea forcefully. "I learned to lean on myself very early on. Penny didn't. True, she has a job and works now. But she doesn't really need to. Basically, she's doing it to keep herself busy until she finds herself a good husband."

The bitterness in Andrea's tone became more and more apparent.

"You don't sound as if you respect Penny much," Olivia couldn't help but comment.

"No, I do respect her. I love Penny. She's a wonderful friend. She has a heart of gold and would do anything for me," Andrea objected.

"And you also work for her father, don't you?" Olivia wanted to find out more.

"Yes, I'm a medical assistant and a good one," claimed Andrea. "Mort was lucky to have me on his staff. I could have gotten a job anywhere."

"I'm sure you could have," said Olivia.

"In fact, Penny wanted me to get the job with her dad. She went all out for me," Andrea remarked.

"And was her father good to you, too?" Olivia's asked in a softer tone.

Andrea paused and played with her hair, twirling it around and around in her fingers again.

"Was he?" Olivia pushed it.

Finally Andrea shrugged. "Mort was good to me in his way, but he was distant. At work he treated me just like everyone else there, not like a part of his family."

Olivia was surprised by the intensity behind Andrea's comment. "Was that okay with you?"

Andrea shrugged. "It was and it wasn't," she uttered. "Of course I wanted him to be more like a dad to me, but he wouldn't."

"That disappointed you?" Olivia felt she was getting close to something important.

"Of course it disappointed me," said Andrea. "It would disappoint you, too, wouldn't it?"

"Naturally." Olivia wanted to keep Andrea talking about it.

Andrea jumped up from the chair then. "It's a relief to hear that! What you're really saying is that I'm not crazy!"

"Who said you were crazy?" Olivia was fascinated.

"Nobody," Andrea answered crisply, "but I can't help wondering that myself from time to time."

"You wonder if you're crazy because you were disappointed by Penny's father?" Olivia dug in.

Andrea got very close to Olivia then, and her voice became raspy. "I think I'm crazy because deep down, unlike everybody else, I never really liked Mort much."

Olivia took a step back, nervously. "Why not?"

"Mort's next door neighbor Margaret doesn't either," Andrea continued, bitterly. "She told me herself. She wouldn't tell everyone, but she told me one night. She said she just wasn't comfortable around him. I was so relieved to hear it."

"Why didn't you like him?" Olivia pushed it. "Why didn't she?"

"Why should I?" Andrea suddenly seemed on the verge of tears.

Olivia remembered Wayne saying that Andrea was jealous of Mort's wife, Christine. "Did your feelings have anything to do with his wife, Christine?"

At that Andrea took a few steps back. "Who said that? Who have you been talking to?"

"I was just wondering," said Olivia.

"You're smart, you're sharp," Andrea burst out. "You can probably see for yourself what a drama queen Christine is, desperate for attention and always flashing her big jewelry in front of anyone who's around."

"Isn't the jewelry part of her own line?" Olivia was confused about why this would bother Andrea.

"No, it's the jewelry Mort gives her, again and again! That's the whole point of it," Andrea insisted. "Christine just wants everyone to see how much Mort loves her, how important she is to him."

Both Olivia and Andrea took a deep breath then at the very same moment.

"Mort loved her a lot more than he cared about you," Olivia whispered almost under her breath.

Andrea heard every word. "Of course he did, that's normal," she exclaimed. "But it's not nice or normal to flaunt things in your face the way Christine did. It's like she wanted everyone else to remember that she was number one, and to stay away from him."

Red lights flashed for Olivia as Andrea kept talking.

"Where were you when Mort was killed?" Olivia asked suddenly.

Andrea stopped and smiled strangely. "You're not asking me if I did it, are you?"

"No, of course not," said Olivia. "It's just a routine part of my job to find out where everyone was at the time of the murder."

Andrea's smile twisted oddly. "Well, actually, I was with Penny all afternoon. There was a storm that day and we went into town to spend the time together shopping."

Perfect alibi, thought Olivia, though she said nothing.

"Did I pass the test? Am I off the hook?" Andrea's eyes narrowed.

"Who said you were ever on the hook?" Olivia responded plainly.

The interview with Andrea left a bitter taste. Andrea seemed to know just what she was doing and saying. Her story and alibi all fit together perfectly, but there were large holes in the picture for Olivia. Who knew what really went on between Andrea and Christine, or even between Andrea and Mort? It was obvious how badly Andrea wanted a father. Had she placed too many hopes for that onto Mort? Or had something actually happened between them that pushed Andrea over the edge? Olivia also thought of the neighbor who didn't like Mort either. Olivia would have to speak to her soon, as well. Under the din of a well-tuned life there were always jarring notes you could hear if you listened closely.

As Olivia took a cab back to the hotel now, she knew Wayne would be there waiting. It was the perfect time to fill each other in and have a late lunch. Olivia hoped all would be easy and natural by now. She even wished the unfortunate encounter between them had never even happened. What had she been thinking? It was just that working on a case took so much of her time, it seemed impossible to include a personal life or the chance to go out and meet others. Olivia would have to find a way to balance that. She wanted and needed the closeness and warmth that a real connection with a man could give her.

To her surprise, when Olivia got back to the hotel, Wayne was outside on a bench in the front, waiting.

"Good to see you," he said when Olivia got out of the cab. "I was just wondering how the interview with Andrea was going."

"Lots to talk about," Olivia answered lightly, smiling. "Let's go to the coffee shop and get something to eat. I don't know about you, but I'm hungry."

*

Olivia and Wayne went to a lovely café in the hotel. To Olivia's surprise, when she entered, the outside of the place was surrounded by trees filled with sparkling lights and little birds flying in them. The atmosphere inside was warm and relaxed. A perfect place to forget your cares. And, thankfully, there were no ruffled feathers and the mood between her and Wayne was pleasant. Nevertheless, Olivia was determined to keep things on track and as professional as possible.

Once they were seated and their orders taken, they looked at each other directly. Wayne seemed a bit sad and also confused. For a split second Olivia wanted to cry, but quickly pushed her emotions to the background. Fortunately they had the case to talk about and she quickly plunged in.

"Andrea is a strange character," Olivia started. "There's a bitter, morose quality about her. She's Penny's best friend, almost like a sister, but she herself was raised by foster parents."

Wayne was glued to every word Olivia was saying. "Did you ask her about her relationship with Christine?"

"Yes, she said Christine flaunted her relationship with Mort, seemed possessive of him. Apparently, according to Andrea, Christine wanted to let everyone know she was number one in his life."

Wayne nodded slowly and smiled. "Common stuff," he said, "not exactly cause for murder."

"Not exactly," Olivia agreed, "but it's worth looking into further. Who knows who else Christine upset? And why she had to be so blatant about her relationship with Mort? By the way, Andrea also commented that she didn't much like Mort and that their next door neighbor Margaret didn't either. So at least there's a little chink in the armor."

"Good." Wayne was pleased to hear it. "You'll talk to Margaret and also Christine soon, I imagine."

"Very soon," said Olivia. "And what did you find at Mort's office?"

"The high point was learning that Andrea was jealous of Christine," said Wayne. "Otherwise, things there seem in good order. There's some money in a personal bank account of Mort's that was not accounted for, but taxes were fully paid on it. Basically, that's common. Nothing else really caught my attention."

"Shouldn't you explore the clinics in Nashville as well, and whatever went on there?" asked Olivia.

"In due time." Wayne seemed thoughtful. "The murder happened down here and the police can be territorial. When they're ready, if they have to, they'll start looking in Nashville as well. They're also waiting to see what happens in Nashville when Mort doesn't return. They're waiting to hear from people down there. See who and what turns up."

"So far nothing?" asked Olivia, fascinated.

"So far things are quiet," replied Wayne. "His clinics down there seem to be taking things in their stride. The good news, of course, is that they've got Hank Waring in custody now, and are bringing him back to town. Nothing will happen until he's investigated. The case will only move forward if he's cleared."

"The police are convinced it's him, aren't they?" Olivia murmured.

"They're sure hoping so," Wayne replied. "In fact, they want us to be at the station first thing tomorrow morning when they'll be grilling him."

"Good," said Olivia.

"That will definitely be a turning point," said Wayne. "Could be the case will be over fast."

"Could be," said Olivia, "but somehow I think we have a long way to go."

"Based on what?" Wayne was interested.

"Based on my gut." Olivia smiled. "This definitely isn't one, big, happy family. Just wait and see what comes out."

*

After lunch was over, Olivia and Wayne walked to the elevator in the lobby together slowly and got in.

"I'm thrilled there are no hard feelings here," Wayne said as they got off on their floor.

"I'm relieved about that as well," said Olivia. "And I'm pleased that at the very least, we're absolutely clear about where we're going and who we are."

CHAPTER NINE

The rain fell in torrents as Olivia and Wayne headed to the police station for Hank Waring's grilling.

"It's good we're here," Wayne remarked. "This way they can't close in on Hank too fast."

"It's nice that they want us to join them," Olivia remarked.

"Yes, it is," Wayne agreed. "These are good guys down here. I'm pleased."

The taxi crawled slowly through the heavy sheets of rain and wind to the station and finally Olivia and Wayne arrived. When they walked up to the front desk they were greeted warmly.

"The interview has actually begun," the clerk behind the desk reported. "Go to Room 343 and take a seat. Not only have you been invited but several other officers and detectives as well."

Olivia was disappointed momentarily. She'd hoped she could interact with the suspect herself.

"We're just going to be in the audience?" she asked Wayne as they walked along the hallway.

"My guess is we'll get a chance to question him eventually," said Wayne.

"Why invite so many to view the interrogation?" Olivia was confused.

"This is big news," Wayne murmured, "and the police probably want to get it out in the press. They're showing what a great job they're doing. They nabbed the convict who ran out of town and are now interviewing him in plain sight."

"In other words it's all a big show?" asked Olivia.

Wayne grimaced. "Possibly, but I'm not sure."

Wayne seemed more subdued than usual, Olivia thought. She wondered what he was really thinking about everything that was going on.

*

The room Hank Waring was being questioned in had about ten cops and detectives sitting in the front row watching the grilling through a one-way window. Olivia and Wayne sat in the third row, right behind them. Chief of Police Joe Dowl was doing most of the questioning, and a young officer Olivia had never seen before sat there as well. He was a rugged, good-looking guy, focusing intensely on every word Dowl had to say.

"Okay, tell me one more time why you were in the vicinity of the crime." Dowl was doing his best to unnerve Hank Waring. Hank looked gaunt and agitated and rubbed his hands together feverishly.

"I told you before. I was taking a walk," Hank uttered.

"Just taking a walk in the middle of the storm?" Dowl shot back quickly.

"The rain let up. I was there after the storm." Hank shook his head back and forth. "I'd been cooped up indoors all day and needed a walk. I was at the Barn before that. People saw me there. I gave you my alibi. It all checked out."

"Yes, it did," the young cop couldn't help but add. "You were having a few beers with Tom Lane, your buddy, at the Barn when Mort Townsend was killed. People saw both of you there."

"What's the Barn?" Olivia whispered to Wayne.

"A well-known pub in town," Wayne replied.

"I was having a few beers," Hank repeated. "That's not a crime, is it?" His face looked gnarled and sad at the same time.

"Of course not," replied the young cop, and Olivia was struck by his compassion.

"You say you were there at the time of death, but as of now the exact time of Townsend's death has only been approximated," Dowl replied. "Your alibi will not check out officially until we get the exact time from the medical examiner."

"And when will that be?" Hank turned his attention to the young officer.

The officer shrugged. He seemed sympathetic to Hank and it surprised Olivia.

"The young cop seems sympathetic to the suspect," she whispered to Wayne. "Who is he?"

"Just some guy on the force," Wayne remarked. "And he's right. Dowl's pushing Hank too hard."

"But Hank fled town, he broke parole," Olivia commented.

"I can understand why," Wayne replied. "He must have panicked. He had to know he'd be caught. In and of itself fleeing town is not evidence of a crime."

"When will you have the exact time of death?" Hank repeated gruffly.

"We should have the report within the next day or so," Dowl responded. "I'll make sure Justin keeps you informed." Dowl motioned to the young cop.

"Once you have the exact time you'll let me go free?" Hank now began to look desperate. "I didn't kill him, I did my time."

"Some people would say once a killer, always a killer," Dowl taunted him.

"I said I didn't do it." Hank's hands turned into fists. "Once you have the exact time of death you'll let me go free?" he repeated

"That's not up to me. You broke your parole, left town," Dowl reminded him. "It was a stupid thing to do."

"He was scared!" Justin interrupted.

"Right! Scared to death," Hank bellowed. "You guys were closing in. I didn't have a chance."

Justin rubbed his face. "There's always a chance," he said.

"Even now?" Hank pushed it. "That's news to me."

"If your alibi holds up, and we find the killer," Justin said.

"My alibi's gonna hold up," Hank insisted. "And that should be enough."

"Will that be enough?" Olivia asked Wayne.

"Could be," Wayne answered. "I don't know what else they have."

"Or am I cooked?" Hank stared into Justin's eyes. To Justin's credit, he didn't flinch, just looked right back.

"No one's cooked," replied Justin.

"That's not true," mused Olivia.

"The kid's doing a good job, though," Wayne said quietly. "He's calming Hank down."

Justin didn't seem like a kid to Olivia. He was about the same age as she was, and Wayne was only a few years older.

"Is Justin misleading Hank?" Olivia wondered out loud.

"Not necessarily," said Wayne.

Olivia found the interaction fascinating between Justin and Hank.

"Listen," Hank piped up loudly now. "Think about it one more time. What reason in the world would I have to take Townsend out? I didn't know the guy. Never saw him in my life."

"You didn't know anybody connected to him either?" Justin pushed on.

"Nobody! Not one of them! And even if I did, what would they have to do with me? I've been rotting in jail for years," Hank added. "I'm a convenient target and that's about it. Pretty easy to nab an old killer and close the case."

"Some killers get a taste for killing and can't wait to do it again," Dowl jumped in. "Some spend years in jail just waiting for the chance to spring again."

"Some, maybe, but not me!" Hank insisted, putting the full force of his attention onto Justin.

Olivia could see why. There was something incredibly sympathetic about Justin, who was listening to every word Hank said.

Justin turned abruptly to Dowl then. "Do you have an idea of when we'll have the exact time of death?"

Dowl shook his head. "If I did I'd have let both of you know," he replied. "But we've got to hold him until we get that information. He's become a flight risk."

"Yeah, hold me all you want," Hank muttered. "But you better keep looking, too. Right now you're empty-handed. Whoever killed Townsend is still out there. And for all you know another victim will turn up soon! If you were smart, you'd let me talk to some of my old buddies in jail. I'll find out if they know something."

"Not a bad idea," Justin said to Dowl.

"All in good time," Dowl replied.

Justin went over to Hank, put his hand on his shoulder, and whispered something in his ear. Hank stood up then and Justin slowly led him out of the interrogation rom. When they were gone, Dowl walked to the one-way window and spoke to those seated outside.

"I'll be right out and Justin will join me, so we can all discuss what just took place."

*

In a few minutes Dowl and Justin walked into the room where the officers and detectives were seated and sat on two high stools up front.

"Thanks for coming," Dowl started. "This is a big case and we need all the input we can get. If anyone has any ideas or noticed something during the interview, don't hold back."

Olivia wondered why Justin was up there with Dowl.

"Nice interview," one of the cops in the front row stated. "But if his alibi checks out, we're back to square one."

"It'll check out," another cop echoed.

"How can you be so sure?" Dowl looked over at him.

"What reason does this guy have to take out Townsend so brutally?" the cop responded.

Olivia could not help but agree. "I'd say focusing on Hank too much is a waste of time," she joined in.

The cops in the front row turned around and all eyes turned to her then. Justin focused in Olivia's direction as well.

"There's a web of relationships that Mort's had," Olivia continued. "Someone involved in them could hold the key."

"Agreed," Justin jumped in, smiling. "It's good to hear someone finally say that flat out."

"It's also good to have Hank in custody," a detective in the front row commented. "We need to give the public something to latch onto while we're searching. It's calming lots of nerves."

"And when the killer strikes again, what good will that do?" another cop interrupted.

Justin shook his head. "The killer's not gonna strike again, not anytime soon, anyhow."

The room got quiet. "How do you know that, buddy?" one of the cops finally asked.

"Who's Justin anyway?" Olivia whispered to Wayne.

"He looks like the bright new rising star on this police force," said Wayne. "He must have solved a few high-profile cases and Dowl's putting him in the limelight. Why do you ask?"

"Just curious," Olivia remarked. "He seems so sure of himself."

"It's easy to be sure of yourself when you're not experienced," Wayne quipped. "It won't last long though. Unexpected hurdles always get thrown in your face."

Olivia was interested in hearing more from Justin. "Why don't you think the killer will strike again?" she addressed him directly.

Justin looked back at her and grinned. "Because the crime was too gruesome," he said. "When you look at the photos, it had to be personal. It was overkill in lots of ways."

"Just what Wayne and I thought," Olivia answered. "Revenge killing, possibly?"

"Yup. Either Townsend cheated someone badly out of money, or it was a love affair that went straight to hell," Justin said.

"That's the direction I'd look in," agreed Olivia.

Justin smiled, pleased. "Well, it's a pleasure to have someone who agrees with me."

Olivia felt Wayne bristle at her side.

"It's time to widen the dragnet," Olivia responded. "I'd say let's go to Nashville where he spent so much of his time. We should see what's happening there."

"That's in the works when the time is right," Dowl answered, taking the reins back in his hands. "Right now, we're waiting for the medical examiner's report. Once Hank's alibi is confirmed, then we'll spread out further."

"Christine's got to be interviewed next," Wayne said to Olivia after they'd left and were walking outside in the balmy air.

"I was just thinking that. I'll do it," said Olivia, glad to have the next steps in place. "And how about you?"

"I like your idea of the investigation spreading out up into Nashville," Wayne commented.

Olivia felt chilled for a moment. "You're thinking of going there yourself and looking around?"

"That would be a smart move," said Wayne. "Frankly, I don't know why they haven't done that already."

"Do you need permission from the police?" asked Olivia.

"Not formally, of course," Wayne answered, "but it's nice to stay on the same page and work together."

Olivia nodded. The thought of Wayne going to Nashville unnerved her somehow.

"We'll stay in close touch," Wayne added. "I won't be gone long."

"I'd wait for the medical examiner's report to come in," said Olivia, "and then it'll be fine with everyone."

Wayne hesitated. "These reports can take longer than you think. And it's always best to go before things cool down."

Olivia couldn't help but agree.

"Let's go take a walk and think it over before we eat," Olivia suggested.

They started to walk and Wayne smiled. "I'll do you one better than that even. Why don't we take a little time to ourselves and take one of the tours of the lighthouse? It'll be fun and relaxing and open our minds."

"I'm open to that." Olivia liked the idea, needed a change of scenery badly.

CHAPTER TEN

Key Biscayne was a world of its own, without the bustle of city life. The tiny island was home to two state parks as well as quiet, palm tree–laced beaches, bike paths, and restaurants. The island also boasted some of the prettiest shores, flanked by sand dunes. In addition to beaches with calm waters, Bill Baggs Cape Florida State Park, on the tip of the island, was home to the towering nineteenth-century Cape Florida Lighthouse. Free guided tours took visitors up the one hundred and nine steps to the top where they could enjoy the scenic 360-degree view.

Olivia and Wayne arrived at the lighthouse just as the next tour was on the way up. There were just a few other people there today. The tour guide spoke about the island and the incredible view they would find when they got to the top.

"You feel as though you're leaving the world behind you," the guide said. "The vistas are breathtaking. And when you return down to earth, you never forget what you saw up there in the clouds."

Olivia smiled. It was a charming way of putting it.

"Nothing wrong with leaving the world behind for a little while," Wayne agreed as they climbed higher and higher. Though it was a bit dizzying, it was also beautiful up there, and definitely mind opening. Standing way above the terrain and gazing all around, Olivia realized how easy it was to get caught in a narrow perspective.

"This is beautiful, magnificent," Wayne said, breathing deeply as he gazed around.

Wayne appreciated life so intensely, Olivia realized again. He was strong, he was stable, and he cared a lot about everyone and everything. What a wonderful combination. But he wasn't available, she had to remind herself again.

"See anything new up here?" Olivia joked.

"I see my better self," Wayne joked back with her. "How about you?"

"I see that everything has a solution," said Olivia, "if we only look at it differently."

Wayne liked that and grew silent for a moment. Olivia walked away from him then, around the viewing tower, entranced by everything.

Suddenly, Wayne came up beside her. "I really hope I didn't hurt your feelings before," he said softly then.

Olivia knew he was referring to the embrace between them that refused to go further.

"No, it's really okay," she replied. "I'm not going to say I wasn't disappointed, but you were just looking at the big picture then, as well."

Wayne smiled sadly. "I was being sensible," he commented. "Relationships are fragile and I certainly don't want to lose all the goodness we have now."

"Of course not," Olivia said. "I don't want to lose it either."

After the tour was over and they returned down to the ground, there was a place close by for a light lunch. Olivia and Wayne went there and while going over the case discussed the idea of his leaving for Nashville for a while. Wayne wanted to explore Mort's connections there. And obviously, it was crucial that this be done sooner than later.

"First call the police and get the okay," Olivia suggested.

"I will. That's my next step," Wayne agreed. "I'll call tonight, after dinner."

*

Fortunately, before Wayne made the call, the medical examiner's report came in late that very afternoon. The time of death was now definite and to the distress of all, Hank Waring's alibi was confirmed. There were no grounds to hold him on. When Wayne called, Dowl picked up and told him the news.

"We're in a new ballpark now," Dowl started. "Hank's alibi is confirmed."

"Perfect timing," Wayne responded. "I was just calling to tell you I want to go down to Nashville and investigate Mort's connections there as soon as possible."

"Great," Dowl agreed instantly. "Go! Only let's keep this as quiet as possible for now. Just between you and me."

"And Olivia, of course," Wayne added.

"Of course," Dowl laughed. "Olivia's your partner, your better half."

"Well, not exactly my better half, not that kind of partner," Wayne balked. "We're work partners only."

"Good." Dowl jumped on it. "It's always better not to mix business and pleasure. I've never seen anything but trouble coming out of that."

Wayne was startled. "It is a slippery slope," he agreed.

"I like you, Wayne," Dowl went on, "you're a good man and a fine detective. You've got a good head on your shoulders. I'd hate to see you taken down by unnecessary complications."

"Of course," Wayne countered. "But just for the record, we're doing great. Olivia's a wonderful partner. She's as smart as a whip."

"I'm sure she is," said Dowl, "just keep it that way."

Wayne thought about the conversation for a while after they hung up. Dowl had suddenly taken a fatherly attitude toward him and it surprised Wayne. His comments also supported what Wayne originally felt. Strangely, it saddened him, too. He'd have to give it more thought.

*

Olivia felt a mixture of relief and unease when Wayne left early the next morning for Nashville. It was good having a partner nearby to check in with about developments. Of course, she could reach him on the phone in a moment, but that was different. And the way they'd left things in their relationship unsettled Olivia as well. On the surface, they'd both behaved in the most mature way possible. They'd been wise, sensible, friendly. But deeper within, Olivia felt rattled and wondered if Wayne felt the same way, too. She couldn't imagine how he couldn't.

Right after breakfast, Olivia put in a call to the Townsend home. Penny answered immediately.

"I need to speak to your mother today," Olivia said. "The investigation has entered another chapter now."

"I know, I know," Penny spoke quickly. "Officer Dowl called and told us the news. He also said you'd be here today to talk to Mom."

That surprised Olivia. Dowl hadn't mentioned to Olivia that he was planning to call Penny and let her know.

"Officer Dowl may even send someone over from the force right after you speak to Mom. This way you can debrief and let them know what you've found out."

Again, Olivia was taken aback that Dowl had told this to Penny and not to her. "Good," she said lightly.

"I also heard that Wayne has headed down to Nashville," Penny went on.

"Sounds like there's nothing in the world you don't know," Olivia tried to respond playfully.

Penny chuckled lightly. "Everything seems to be different now that they have to let Hank Waring go. The heat's on to find more suspects."

"Seems so," Olivia agreed. "Okay, I'll be at your place in about half an hour," she said. "Is that okay with you?"

"Perfect," Penny replied.

Olivia noticed that Penny had many different sides to her. She could be very easy to talk to at one time, and completely rattled the next. That was to be expected, of course, in circumstances like this. Basically Olivia liked Penny.

*

Olivia arrived at the Townsend home in about half an hour. It was good to get there at short notice, she thought. That way there would not be enough time for Christine to really pull herself together. It was always much better to catch a person at least half by surprise. There would be less chance that way for Christine to present her well-formed façade. Especially with Christine, this element of surprise was needed.

As Olivia expected, when she entered the home, Christine was ready and waiting for her. Dressed in velvet lounging slacks and a tunic, she was seated grandly on the sofa in the living room, an air of high expectancy surrounding her.

"Thank you so much for your time," Olivia said as she walked over to her and sat down.

"Of course, of course," said Christine. "But for starters, I just want you to know that it was not my idea to hire either you or your partner."

Olivia was taken aback. Was Christine opposed to having them on the case?

"The idea was completely Penny's and my guess is she roped Lance in to it." Christine ran her well-manicured hand through her hair. She was extremely well cared for and startlingly lovely for a woman her age, thought Olivia.

"Both Penny and Lance only want to do the best for you and everybody," Olivia responded.

Christine smiled wanly. "Naturally, that's both true and entirely beside the point," she replied. "I'm the one in charge. And more than ever now that Mort is gone." At that her voice caught in her throat, betraying her effort to seem on top of things.

"This must be very hard for you." Olivia immediately decided to ignore Christine's elaborate presentation and address her shaky feelings.

"Of course it's hard," Christine said in an imperious tone. "How could it not be? Actually, it's totally impossible to believe that my husband is gone."

"Naturally," Olivia echoed, remembering that this woman was as much a victim as Mort. "Fortunately, your children are close and will help with everything."

"Yes, they are." Christine took that up quickly. "Even my son Thomas, who lives abroad. Despite what anyone tells you, he is close to me as well. He doesn't have to live next door either, to prove it."

"You're in touch with him regularly?" Olivia was surprised.

"Not regularly." Christine breathed heavily. "But often enough."

"Does he know about his father's death?"

"Not yet." Christine's eyes closed briefly and she looked for a moment as if she were about to swoon at the reminder that Mort was dead. "But he will soon. What's the need for telling him immediately? Mort is gone. It's over."

Olivia found her reaction unusual and interesting. "Was Thomas close to his father?" she asked.

"Thomas was close to no one in this family except me," Christine retorted. "And Mort didn't really care either. Mort had plenty of people he was close to. He used to laugh about Thomas, actually. He'd say, one down and two up! Meaning two of his children were close to him and one not. He took it in stride."

"He was realistic?" Olivia asked, pleased that they were talking about Mort now.

"Yes." Christine wet her lips and smiled a bit. "That's actually a good word to describe him. Mort was very realistic about many things. And, of course, about other things, not at all!"

Olivia felt as if she were in a house of mirrors with Christine. Everything she presented could be looked at in many different ways at once.

"Did you love your husband?" Olivia tried to break through and get a direct, blunt answer.

Christine looked entirely startled. "What a bizarre question!" she replied. "Outrageous, actually. Of course I loved Mort, he was a great husband. In fact, he was known for being a great husband. Ask anyone. He did everything right. You couldn't have asked for anyone better."

Olivia noticed perspiration start to form on Christine's face.

"It's unusual to be so happy in a long marriage," Olivia said softly.

Christine perked up at that. "What's so unusual about it?"

"Inevitably areas of difference arise," Olivia murmured.

"How would you know? You're just a child," Christine spat back at her. "And this generation knows nothing about commitment either, do they?"

"It's all part of my training," Olivia answered, calmly. She was determined not to go on a roller coaster ride with this volatile woman.

Christine stood up off the couch then, smoothed out her clothing, and looked at Olivia harshly. "Well, if you must know the truth, even though we were definitely very happy, actually I was getting a bit bored recently. And Mort was changing too. He was getting stricter, more pig-headed about things."

This was just what Olivia was looking for, a taste of reality. "How was Mort stricter?"

"I just mean he'd become more adamant about things. For example, I wanted to grow my jewelry business, and he wouldn't let me." The memories seem to be flooding Christine now.

"Really? Why not?"

"Mort kept saying enough was enough. He didn't want me flitting all over selling my jewelry, constantly looking for exposure," she replied. Then Christine suddenly spun around toward Olivia. "At first I thought he was jealous of the attention I was getting, but then I realized he wasn't. And also, it wasn't a matter of whether I wanted to grow my business! I told him I had to. Mort had been bringing home less and less money recently."

Olivia trembled at the force of her vehemence. This was important. "Why was he bringing home less money? Trouble with the clinics?"

"No." Christine looked away. "The clinics are flourishing."

"So, where was the money going?" Olivia was alerted.

"Good question, my dear." Christine began pacing around the room slowly. "I asked Mort that over and over again. He simply said there were lots of people who needed money in the world and it was his responsibility to help them. In fact, he said it was his honor to. Naturally I took exception to that."

"Was he talking about giving more to charity?" asked Olivia.

"Of course, that's what he was implying," Christine answered. "Mort was involved with many charities over his lifetime."

"Did you object to that?"

"Of course not," Christine said. "Not if I had all I needed as well."

"You didn't have all you needed recently?" Olivia asked.

At that Christine flushed. "I can't put it that way, exactly," she snapped. "I mean, look around, I have plenty of things. But not as much as I used to."

"You wanted more from him?" Olivia hung on to this line of questioning relentlessly. She wanted to break through and get a real feel for what went on in Mort's life. And between him and his outlandish wife.

But Christine suddenly paused, alarmed to realize what she was saying. "What are you really asking me?" she said.

"I need to know all about Mort," Olivia answered softly. "It will help us understand what really happened to him."

"He was killed on the beach," Christine shot back forcefully. "Right before the storm started."

"What was he doing there?" Olivia became forceful as well.

"He was taking a walk, he had a right to," said Christine.

"Was it something he did regularly?" Olivia persisted.

"Of course, why not? Nothing wrong with that." Christine wasn't budging.

"Nothing's wrong, of course," said Olivia. "But who knew he would be there? How did they know it?"

"That's the question, isn't it?" Christine grew pale. "We all thought it was a random killing at first."

"Hank Waring's been exonerated now," Olivia reminded her.

"Not exonerated exactly," Christine breathed. "His alibi holds up, that's all."

Olivia took a deep breath and dove in. "Christine," she asked emphatically, "was Mort faithful to you?"

Christine's eyebrows rose and her hands stiffened as she pointed at Olivia.

"Absolutely," she practically shouted. "Mort was totally faithful all these years. And don't you dare say anything else to anyone."

Suddenly the doorbell rang loudly. "Who's that?" Christine seemed alarmed. "Penny," she started calling.

"It's okay, Mom," Penny called back. "It's the police officer they said would come over after you had a chance to talk to Olivia."

Christine made a quick dash out of the living room. "You talk to him all you want," she said to Olivia. "As for me, I've had enough for today. There's nothing more I have to tell you."

CHAPTER ELEVEN

Justin sauntered into the living room just as Christine was departing. "Hey, I'm Justin Hartley," he said, walking over to Olivia boldly.

Olivia turned around and was suddenly face to face with him. Justin had an electric energy. He was handsome, alert, and also a bit edgy.

"Hi," Olivia replied, "I remember seeing you at Hank Waring's interview."

"Good memory," Justin responded, pleased.

It was good to have someone here to talk to, not only about Christine, but the case in general. "I'm glad you're here," said Olivia.

"Thanks," said Justin. "I'm glad to be here, too. I just had a useful talk with Penny. Did you finish up with Christine?"

"Yes," said Olivia. "This was my first meeting with her."

"Christine's been hard to talk to," Justin responded. "The guys on the force have tried a few times."

"It was too soon before this," said Olivia. "Christine hasn't been ready until now."

"Do you mind telling me what you found out?" Justin's sharp blue eyes glistened as he took a step closer.

"Certainly," said Olivia. "I'd be glad to."

"You never know who's listening in the house. We can talk here, or go to a nearby spot outside," Justin offered.

"I was planning to spend more time with Penny this morning," Olivia replied, not wanting to leave the house with him. Once Olivia left, Penny might think their time together was over and leave as well.

"Sure, let's talk here then," said Justin, going to a leather chair in the corner of the room and pulling another one close for her.

Olivia liked his take-charge attitude, and his willingness to respect her wishes. It was also interesting to see how he could change his plan of action on a dime. Olivia enjoyed working with the police. She learned something new from every one of them.

"I was officially put on the case a day ago," Justin remarked, as Olivia sat down beside him.

"Congratulations," said Olivia. "Have you been on the force long?"

"A little over a year," he replied. "I like what you're doing better though. I'm thinking of becoming a detective myself. It's exciting to me and a natural next step."

Olivia smiled. She knew just how he felt. Justin was upbeat and exciting to be with. And it was nice to be with someone the same age as her.

"I always knew that Hank didn't kill Townsend." Justin was enjoying talking.

"How did you know that?" Olivia was interested.

"I think the others knew, too," Justin went on. "I could see that the police felt good about having a high-profile suspect, though. So most couldn't voice any doubt about him. I especially appreciated it when you said at the interview that you didn't think Hank was the killer, too."

"I'm glad," said Olivia.

"Have any ideas about who did it?" Justin leaned closer.

"Not yet, of course," Olivia replied.

"No one in mind?" Justin pushed a bit.

"I'm not the kind who jumps to conclusions," said Olivia.

"Good," said Justin. "That's smart. How about that guy you were with?"

"My partner, Wayne, is down in Nashville now, exploring," she said.

"Really?" Justin was surprised. "That's a good move. Who is he exactly, your husband, too?"

Olivia felt alarmed by the idea of Wayne being her husband. "Wayne's my business partner," she replied. "Wells and Darrington, Private Investigators."

"Very cool, very nice." Justin smiled warmly at her.

"Thanks," said Olivia. "Now, what do you want to know about Christine?"

"Whatever you want to tell me." Justin grinned. "I heard she's a real prima donna."

Olivia didn't like Christine being referred to as a prima donna. It was disrespectful.

"Christine's a grieving wife who's definitely flashy," Olivia replied, suddenly feeling protective of her.

"So, did she give you any worthwhile leads?" Justin seemed hungry to take action.

"Not really," said Olivia, wanting to slow him down and also not wanting to spill all the beans. Olivia didn't know if Justin could handle the nuances of her interview with Christine sensitively enough.

"Christine told me that she and Mort had an excellent marriage," Olivia continued. "Obviously they have a close family."

"Nothing's obvious in our line of work," Justin shot back. "I heard there's a son who's been estranged from the family for a while."

"Thomas," said Olivia. "He's actually close to his mother and lives abroad. He hasn't even heard about his father's murder yet."

"That's weird," said Justin. "Why not?"

"I don't think it amounts to much," Olivia replied.

"What else did you find out?" Justin couldn't take his eyes off her.

"Christine has a thriving jewelry business." Olivia stuck to surface information.

"Yeah, sure, we all know that," he said.

Once again Olivia clammed up. She didn't know how Justin would handle the fact that Christine had grown bored and restless, or that Mort hadn't wanted her to grow her business. Before Olivia gave sensitive details to the police, she needed more information herself. Otherwise, they could jump on what she told them, barge in, question people roughly, and cause everyone to close up.

"What else can you tell me?" Justin had a relentless energy.

"Christine insisted that Mort was faithful to her," Olivia said swiftly then. "That eliminates a possible revenge killing from a spurned lover."

"It doesn't eliminate anything," Justin bounced back. "Everybody insists they're faithful, but how many really are?"

Olivia was struck by Justin's bluntness and insight. She wondered what she could tell him that would help everyone. Suddenly she hit on it.

"And it seems that Mort wasn't bringing home as much money as before," she said then. "This is probably something for the forensic accountants to explore."

"We've got a team of them checking out all the finances," Justin filled her in. "That's it?" He sounded disappointed.

"This was only my first meeting with Christine," said Olivia. "I had to go slow and be careful."

Justin gave Olivia an intense glance. "But you don't seem like someone who goes slow and is careful," he remarked.

Olivia didn't know how to take that. "I am very careful with the families of victims," she replied. "They're steeped in pain and trauma."

"That's right, they are. Good for you." Justin quieted down.

"What about you? Is there something new you can tell me?" Olivia wanted to take charge of the discussion now. "Any other suspects the police are looking at?"

"No, not yet," he answered. "But I'm really glad that your partner left for Nashville. I've been pushing the force to spread out up there for a while. They've been dragging their heels. Basically, they haven't wanted to share the case with the Nashville authorities. Probably want all the glory for themselves. But now they have to, and plan to shortly."

"Good," said Olivia, standing up.

"I guess that's it then?" Justin looked disappointed.

"I'm sorry I don't have something more dramatic," said Olivia.

"No, I don't mean to imply that," said Justin. "I just mean there's a lot more for all of us to do. Actually, it's been really good having the chance to talk to you. It's like a breath of fresh air."

Olivia liked that. She finally relaxed a moment and smiled. "You too," she said. "It's always good to get a new take on things."

"Not only good, it's essential," Justin quipped. "And I've got all the guys on the force to talk to, but right now, you're here alone."

Olivia took exception to that. "I'm not alone at all," she insisted. "I can talk to Wayne any time I want to on the phone. And we do all the time."

"That's true, of course," said Justin. "But it's important to talk face to face as well."

"Of course." Olivia couldn't deny that.

Justin stood up then, smiled broadly, and got ready to go. "Hope I see you soon," he said as he got to the door. "We're all here for you. Stay in touch."

*

After Justin left, Olivia sat in the living room alone for a few minutes. Her time with both Christine and Justin had been jarring for her. It would be good to talk to Penny, and hopefully Lance was somewhere around as well. Lance was always clear and calming. Quite a bit of time had passed since Olivia arrived and she hoped Penny hadn't gone out. She needed more time with her and wanted it now. Thankfully, just as Olivia was about to get up and look for her, Penny herself walked into the living room.

"Everybody gone?" asked Penny in a soft tone.

Olivia nodded. "Yes, they have. I was hoping to spend a little more time with you."

"That's great." Penny smiled. "I'm glad you're here Olivia, I really am."

"Me too," Olivia replied.

"There's some lunch in the kitchen," Penny said. "If you're hungry we can go there to talk and eat."

"Good idea," said Olivia. She was hungry and also eager to move around and get a better sense of the home Mort had lived in, and the world he'd occupied.

"Did you have a good talk with Officer Hartley?" Penny asked, as they walked through the hallway. "I heard he's a real crackerjack."

"He's definitely all set to go," said Olivia, as they walked into the large, beautifully tiled kitchen at the side of the home. The kitchen was bright and sunny, with a large round wooden table on which platters of sandwiches, salad, and chips were spread out.

"Are you expecting a lot of people again today?" asked Olivia, looking at the food.

"Lance ordered the food just in case," said Penny. "But thankfully, the crowds are thinning down. Soon my father will have a small private cremation and a memorial later on."

"How are you really handling all this?" asked Olivia.

Penny sat down at the kitchen table then and suddenly became limp. "I'm not handling it," she whispered. "I rally for a little while and then it hits me again."

"Is your brother here? Is anyone else in the family around?" asked Olivia, concerned about her.

"Lance had to go out to do a few things," said Penny, "and my Uncle Angie did too. Uncle Angie will be back soon."

"It's good for your mother that Angie's around," said Olivia.

"Definitely," Penny agreed. "Uncle Angie's a forceful guy. He takes good care of her, doesn't let her go off the deep end."

"Was Angie close to your father, too?" asked Olivia.

"Not so much," said Penny. "I mean of course they were on good terms, but guys don't usually get so close. My mother was always Uncle Angie's main focus."

Olivia nodded.

"Have a sandwich," said Penny then.

Olivia reached out for a small egg salad sandwich on fresh whole grain bread.

"How did your talk go with my mother?" asked Penny as Olivia began to eat.

"We had a good first meeting," said Olivia, hungrier than she had realized.

"My mother can be tough, there's no question about it," said Penny. "That's why I called you and Wayne on the case."

"Yes, I remember, that's the first thing you mentioned," Olivia replied.

"My mom gets so upset and even nasty at times. I thought having her own private investigators around would calm her down."

"Has it?" asked Olivia.

"Frankly, I don't think she even takes it in at this point," said Penny. "She's shaken to the core. The truth is complicated. My mother isn't someone you can really talk to, or tell your deepest secrets to," Penny continued.

Olivia could certainly understand that. Christine seemed mostly concerned about herself.

"My friend Andrea is someone I can really talk to though," Penny continued.

"You're lucky to have such a close friend," said Olivia.

Penny reached for a sandwich herself. "I know I am," she whispered. "Andrea's been helping me with this for a while."

"What do you mean a while?" Olivia was confused. "Your father only died a short time ago."

"Can I talk to you, too, Olivia?" Penny's head shot up then and she stared straight at her.

"Of course," said Olivia. "That's what I'm here for."

"Actually, I'd been having strange dreams the whole month before my father was killed," Penny blurted out then, biting into the bread.

Olivia stopped eating. "Dreams about what?" she asked carefully.

"I dreamt someone was out to get my father." Penny's voice lowered. "Actually, it was terrifying. I kept having the same dream again and again."

Olivia shuddered.

"I told my mother about the dreams but she scoffed at me. She said it's nonsense to pay attention to dreams. Now I wish I hadn't listened to her." Penny began trembling. "I blame myself."

Olivia put her hand on Penny's shaking hand. "You can't blame yourself for this," she said. "It's a temptation to do that, but don't. From the looks of it, you're a fantastic daughter."

"But I should have listened to my dreams. Andrea told me to listen. I told her about them, too," Penny added.

"How could you have listened? What could you have done?" Olivia wondered what Andrea had in mind.

"I don't know, but I could have stayed closer to home. I could have watched who came and went more carefully. Andrea told me to watch who came and went. I didn't do it, though."

"Really?" Olivia was shocked. "Why did Andrea suggest that?"

"Because of my dreams," Penny repeated. "Andrea believes in dreams, totally."

"Well, think back now." Olivia picked up on it. "Who exactly came and went?"

"I don't know, I'm not sure, I wasn't here a lot." Penny suddenly began wailing.

This was a dangerous road to go down and Olivia realized it. But she decided to take another step on it, anyhow.

"What do you think Andrea was talking about? What was the danger? Who could have possibly showed up at your house?"

"I have no idea," Penny insisted, "but I also kept dreaming of a woman, dressed in pale blue. She kept appearing again and again in my dreams."

Olivia suddenly had trouble swallowing. Oddly enough, she and Wayne had recently talked about dreams. He paid them little attention, but Olivia felt differently. She herself had many repetitive dreams the weeks before Paul, her first fiancé, had died.

"You kept seeing a woman in blue?" Olivia now asked intently.

"Yes, a woman in blue with golden blonde hair," Penny elaborated.

"Was she someone your father could have possibly been involved with?" Olivia had to ask.

"I don't think so. But how do I know?" Penny began to get frantic again. "That was my dream!"

"What did Andrea say about it?" Olivia felt herself getting pulled in.

"Andrea said search for the woman in blue, Penny! How could I search for a woman in blue? I decided right then to call you instead." Penny's voice grew raspy.

"You did the right thing," Olivia insisted.

"To search for a woman based on a dream is crazy, isn't it?" Penny grew shakier.

Olivia didn't know how to answer. "It's certainly not something we normally do," she replied.

"It's crazy, it's crazy." Penny started crying now. "I'm losing my mind. We all are."

"No, it's okay," declared Olivia. "It's normal to think all kinds of things when someone you love dies this way. Especially when you've had dreams like that for a whole month before."

Penny put her head in her hands then and started sobbing softly. "Thank you, thank you," she managed between sobs.

Olivia slowly pushed herself back from the table.

"Don't go, please." Penny's head shot up. "My Uncle Angie will be back any minute. I'd really like you to talk to him. I'm going to my room in the house to rest now," Penny said. "You can just wait in the kitchen and he'll come right in."

CHAPTER TWELVE

After Penny left, Olivia took another small sandwich and some salad and began to eat slowly. She couldn't get the image of a woman in blue out of her mind. Even though it was just a dream image, it was intriguing. Who knew what Penny might have inadvertently seen, what had struck her and lodged within? Olivia always thought that dreams held reservoirs of meanings that few had any idea of. She remembered how she'd dreamt of Paul leaving for weeks before his cancer claimed him. Night after night she would dream of him walking down a long golden corridor. Once, in the dream, she even tried to run after him, but he'd stopped her forcefully.

"You're not coming with me, even if you want to," Paul had told her powerfully before disappearing from sight. "You have too much work to do here."

Olivia reached for a bottle of ginger ale that was also on the table. Just as she began to pour the soda into a paper cup, she heard a noise behind her.

"This must be Olivia," a growly voice uttered from behind.

Olivia turned to see Angie standing there, peering in.

"Yes, it's me." Olivia stood up.

"Penny texted me and told me you'd be here in the kitchen waiting to speak to me," Angie went on. He was wearing jeans and a navy shirt, looking dapper. "Should I come in and join you for lunch, or should we take a walk outside?" he asked.

"Come on in," said Penny, glad to see him. The morning was turning out to be chock-full of people to talk to. Even though she did not yet know how it would all come together, Olivia realized that a tapestry of Mort's life was being woven together for her.

"Christine's my baby sister and there's nothing I wouldn't do to take care of her," Angie informed Olivia in a no-nonsense tone, as he sat down. "I'll be staying here at the house with her for an unknown period of time now."

Olivia wondered if Angie had a family or job of his own, but hesitated to ask.

"You don't feel Christine's safe alone?" she asked.

"She's not." Angie was emphatic as he grabbed two sandwiches and threw them on a plate. "No one has the least idea

69

yet about who killed Mort. Or if they're after Christine, too. And if you ask me, they'll never know."

"Why not?" Olivia felt personally challenged.

"Because this lousy killing was either a totally random job done by some nut who's long gone from town, or something has been going on in Mort's life that no one has the slightest idea of. Either way, how's the truth going to surface?"

"That's what I'm here for," said Olivia boldly.

Angie laughed. "Forgive me for laughing, honey," he said, "but it's going to take a lot more than a young, beautiful woman poking around in our corners."

Olivia decided to stay neutral in response to Angie's tough comment.

"You can't be sure of that," she responded. "There are harder cases than this one that have been cracked. And I've been involved in cracking them."

"I'm sure there are." Angie was taken aback momentarily. "And I certainly didn't mean to make light of your work. But even if you're the best you can get in your line of work, this is a totally senseless killing."

They were all senseless killings, thought Olivia, no matter what the supposed motive was.

"What do you think happened to Mort?" Olivia decided to turn it back on Angie.

"Frankly, I have no idea. None at all," said Angie. "This came totally out of the blue for us all."

"You never ever suspected anything?" Olivia kept at it.

"What was there to suspect? Mort was a fine guy, he lived his life."

"The two of you were close?" Olivia wanted details.

"Not especially," Angie answered truthfully. "Why should we be? He was good to my sister and that was enough."

"And it didn't bother Mort at all that you were so close to his wife?"

"Just the opposite." Angie grinned at the thought of it. "He was happy about it. Mort enjoyed seeing Christine busy. He also enjoyed time to himself. He needed it, if you ask me."

Olivia took that in. "Many men would be jealous of their wives being very close to another family member," she added, waiting to see how Angie would react.

Angie just shook his head. "Nah, not Mort. I just told you, he liked plenty of time to himself."

Olivia wondered about that. "What did he do with that time?"

"How would I know?" answered Angie. "You know, even though he was happy with everyone, he held a lot close to the vest. Mort was a private guy, basically."

Olivia found that interesting and suddenly thought of the woman in blue. As far-fetched as it seemed she had to pursue it further.

"Is it possible Mort was secretly involved with someone on the side?" she continued.

"Of course it's possible, anything's possible." Angie rolled his eyes. "Guys have been known to do things like that before, haven't they? It doesn't usually get them killed, though."

"I'm not speaking hypothetically." Olivia got tougher. "Do you have any knowledge of something like that going on in Mort's life? Was there another woman?"

Angie paused for a long moment. Too long, Olivia thought. "A long time ago, maybe," Angie answered. "But over the years when I knew him, no."

"What happened a long time ago?" Olivia was intrigued.

"Is this really important? Does it really matter?" Angie was reluctant to take it further. "People do things when they're young and then they grow up and forget about them."

"Of course it's important," Olivia answered swiftly. "Whatever you tell me about Mort adds to the picture. If you want to find his killer, speak up."

"It was just before Mort and my sister got married." Angie's voice dropped low. "You're sure this is going to make a difference?"

"I'm not sure," Olivia answered frankly, "but tell me, and I'll let you know."

"Mort cheated on my sister right before the wedding. It was with someone he'd dated before. Just a last-minute fling, something like that. I'm sure bachelors do it all the time. It's a way of saying good-bye to their freedom, one last blast."

Olivia cringed. "How do you know about this?"

"I happened to find out about it from the woman's girlfriend," said Angie. "The girlfriend was even more upset than you are right now. She thought Christine should call off the marriage. I thought that was complete nonsense."

"You told Christine, of course?" asked Olivia.

"Of course I didn't," Angie proclaimed. "Why would I? You think I wanted to break my sister's heart?"

"Wasn't it her right to know and her choice about whether she wanted to go on with the marriage?" Olivia was disturbed.

"It was her right to be happy with the man she loved," Angie proclaimed. "Guys make mistakes all the time, honey. That's no reason to tear their lives apart."

"So you didn't tell Christine about it?"

"I didn't talk to Christine, but I did talk to Mort. I gave him hell, actually. He swore again and again he wouldn't repeat it. He said he didn't know what came over him, begged me not to tell Christine. I promised that I wouldn't. And I never did. I'm a man of my word."

Olivia felt heartsick hearing the story. It reminded her of Todd sleeping with an old girlfriend just as he and Olivia were getting engaged. Did this really happen regularly? Was there no one who could be trusted?

"So there, now you have the story," Angie continued. "Feel any better because of it? Do you know anything more about who could have killed Mort now?"

Angie was mocking her and Olivia felt it. She decided to remain completely professional.

"One piece after another completes the puzzle," she remarked simply. "You never know where any piece of information will lead."

"You're not going to tell my sister either, are you?" Angie's face suddenly turned red. "I sure hope you aren't, or honey, I don't know what I would do. But I tell you it wouldn't be pretty."

"Are you threatening me, Angie?" Olivia got tight.

"I'm not threatening, just warning," he barked. "Do you plan on telling Christine?"

"No, of course not," Olivia spoke strongly. "It happened too many years ago."

*

Fortunately, Angie left shortly and Olivia decided to go back to the hotel and unwind. The morning had been strangely grueling and she needed time to process what had happened.

On the way back in the cab, Olivia's phone rang. She picked up immediately, and as she hoped, thankfully, Wayne was on the other end.

"How's it going?" Wayne asked, seemingly pleased that she answered.

"What an intense morning," Olivia breathed.

"Really? I wish I'd been there. Anything new?" he replied.

"I spoke to Christine, her brother Angie, and also the police sent that young cop Justin over to see what I'd found out."

"Justin? Why?" Wayne sounded slightly miffed.

"They're just keeping connected to what we're doing," said Olivia, "and also letting me know I've got all the support I need while you're out of town."

"That's a bit presumptuous, I'd say," Wayne responded. "I'm just a phone call away."

"They mean well," Olivia insisted. "How about you? What's it like there? Anything to report?"

"Not yet," Wayne said. "I've just settled in and am about to visit the head administrator at the clinic down here."

"Wonderful," said Olivia. "Please let me know how it goes along."

"Of course I will," Wayne answered briskly. "I always do, don't I?"

"Yes, you do, you're great at that," said Olivia.

"Thanks," said Wayne, quietly, a tinge of emotion in his voice. "At least I'm great at something."

CHAPTER THIRTEEN

Nashville was beautiful, warm, alive, exciting, the capital of Tennessee and home to Vanderbilt University and legendary country music. Honky-tonks lined the streets, alive with music. As Wayne walked along the trendy streets, he felt the whole place rocking. Olivia would love it here, he thought as he headed downtown to Mort's clinics. It almost felt odd to be here without Olivia. He'd gotten so used to working together, it was like part of him was missing.

Wayne picked up his pace. It was good to be here alone, he quickly reminded himself. The skies were bright blue and there was a softness in the air that relaxed him. He'd needed the break. Things had gone too far too fast between him and Olivia. Fortunately, both had come to their senses and pulled back into professional mode. Wayne knew it was the right decision too, especially as he so strongly felt her absence now.

As Wayne got closer to the clinic, he paused and looked around. Since he'd spoken to Olivia on the phone, he'd been uneasy. It bothered him that Justin turned up right after he'd left town. Of course it was routine; the police sent him to check on things. But Wayne didn't like it anyhow. Olivia hadn't said too much about it, either. Maybe the guy probably hadn't made much of an impression.

Or, of course, it was entirely possible that the opposite was true. It could have been that Olivia thought the world of Justin. Wayne knew that Olivia was prone to jumping into relationships quickly, especially exciting ones. She'd done exactly that with her second fiancé, Todd. She'd never even looked into his background. Wayne thought about how he and Olivia met when he'd been assigned to investigate Todd's shocking murder. Even though Olivia had been devastated she'd been amazingly strong, determined to jump in and help. Now Olivia had grown into a truly professional detective. The work was good for her, and she was amazing at it, too. It startled Wayne to realize how much had changed for both of them in such a short period of time.

Wayne now turned the corner and arrived at the long, low building that Mort's clinic was housed in. It was fascinating to notice the way Mort had duplicated his health care model and how well they were doing both in Nashville and in Key Biscayne. Wayne's appointment with Len Radson, the chief administrator, was scheduled for ten minutes from now. Wayne had arrived just in time.

Wayne entered the building and walked directly to the office number he'd been given and knocked on the closed door.

The door opened promptly and a tall, formal, well-dressed man in his late forties stood there looking at Wayne carefully.

"Len Radson?" asked Wayne.

"Yes, that's right," the man said. "Wayne Darrington, I assume?"

"Exactly," said Wayne.

"Good, please come in." Len ushered Wayne into a beautifully decorated room with wooden file cabinets lining one wall, and a large conference table in the center.

"Quite an impressive operation you have here," Wayne said, as they sat down opposite one another.

"All of this is thanks to Mort," Len responded. "He was the brains behind everything. And he was responsible for finding the cutting-edge treatments."

"It's a terrible loss," Wayne replied.

"That's putting it mildly," said Len. "And people are just barely beginning to find out about it, as well. Naturally, they're in total shock."

"Naturally," said Wayne.

"I just found out myself. All I knew in the beginning was that Mort hadn't shown up. I've only told a few people here the whole truth. Mort didn't like personal information about his life to be discussed. He even kept his clinics in Nashville and Key Biscayne separate. We hardly talked to each other at all."

"I'm really sorry," said Wayne. "I'm sure Mort was liked by all."

"Absolutely," Len spoke definitively. "Why did it take so long to let us know and have the investigation branch out into Nashville?"

"The murder took place in Key Biscayne," said Wayne. "The search always first centers in the location of the crime. At first the police thought they had the killer. They were waiting to be sure before moving forward. And probably they were also waiting to see what surfaced by itself in Nashville when Mort didn't return."

"This is horrible, awful, gruesome!" Len exclaimed. "We saw each other all the time Mort was here. He checked in with me every day. Mort trusted me."

"Did he spend a lot of time in the office when he was in Nashville?" Wayne continued.

"As much time as needed," Len answered crisply. "Mort had a lot to do to oversee the clinics. When he came to Nashville he was here, there, and everywhere."

"Where? Where did he go? What did he do?" Wayne was interested.

Len suddenly looked ruffled. "I didn't follow him around exactly." His tone suddenly turned scruffy. "And I didn't ask him personal questions, either. He wouldn't have liked that at all."

Obviously, Len didn't like that he was being asked personal questions either, thought Wayne.

"Why not?" asked Wayne, perplexed.

"He wasn't the kind of guy you'd ask personal questions to," was all Len would reply.

"Well, even if you didn't ask Mort personal questions, I'm sure you were familiar with his schedule?" Wayne wouldn't be stopped.

"Sometimes I was, sometimes I wasn't," Len responded. "Mort was a private guy. He told me what he had to. And I let it go at that. That's why we did well together. I took him at face value."

This was the first time Wayne had heard that Mort was a private guy. That wasn't the impression he'd had of him in Key Biscayne. Actually, Wayne had heard the opposite, that Mort was a pillar of the community, a great father, husband, and very socially engaged.

"What do you mean he was private?" Wayne had to take this further. "Mort was secretive?"

"No. He was private, quiet!" said Len. "His business was his. He wasn't blasting it all over town. He liked time alone, too. Sometimes he'd be off the grid for a whole day."

"Why?" Wayne felt uneasy. It was almost as if two different people were being described.

"Why not?" Len adamantly defended him. "We all need downtime, don't we?"

"Some more than others," Wayne commented. "Some don't like it at all, can't be alone. Some need lots of company. That was my impression of Mort."

"Well, you were wrong. That wasn't him," grumbled Len. "Sometimes Mort would be in the mood for company, but not often. Other times he'd suddenly turn quiet and remote."

"What was bothering him?" Wayne's voice lowered.

"I wouldn't say something was bothering Mort," Len replied. "He had a lot on his mind, that's for sure. And he wasn't about to talk to everyone about it."

Wayne wondered what Mort had on his mind and who, if anyone, he spoke to about it.

"What did Mort do for fun?" Wayne tried another tack now, feeling increasingly uncomfortable. Either Len was hiding something, or Wayne was being overly sensitive.

"Mort didn't come to Nashville for fun, exactly. He came to work." Len looked ruffled.

"Wait a minute." Wayne leaned closer to him suddenly. "Something's off here. Mort Townsend was brutally murdered a short time ago. I need every bit of information about him I can possibly get. I want to know where he went, who he interacted with, where he went to sleep at night. Did he have his own apartment here? Did he stay in a hotel?"

Len stiffened and became silent.

"If you don't cooperate you're obstructing an investigation," Wayne informed him. "And, frankly, I don't understand it. I would think you would want to tell me whatever you know. Don't we have the same goal here? To find the killer?"

Len balked. "Of course, I want to find the killer as much as you do," he said.

"So, what's the hold-back?" Wayne felt himself growing upset.

"Mort lived a good life and now he's gone. He did good work and had a fine reputation," Len spoke ponderously. "He deserves his privacy, doesn't he?"

"Not anymore," Wayne shot back at him. "Not after he was brutally murdered."

"He did nothing to deserve it, though," Len insisted.

"We don't really know that, do we?" Wayne countered. "Are you worried about what's going to come out about him?"

"I don't like to see people's lives trashed and slandered," said Len. "Mort still deserves respect no matter how he died."

"And he'll get it," Wayne insisted. "We're giving him a lot more respect by finding his killer than brushing important things under the rug."

"That's true." Len faltered a moment. Then he stood up swiftly and walked to a filing cabinet nearby. He reluctantly took an envelope out of the top drawer and slowly walked back to Wayne.

"What's that?" asked Wayne, staring at the envelope that Len slowly handed him.

"There's an address inside. Go there," Len murmured. Then he turned his back on Wayne abruptly and walked out of the room.

Wayne opened the envelope slowly. Inside was an address scrawled on a piece of paper. What's this? Wayne wondered. Of course the only way to know was to go there immediately, knock on the door, and find out.

*

The taxi took Wayne to a lovely, small home on a cul de sac in a residential area of Nashville. The house was surrounded by trees, and a winding cobblestone pathway led up to the front door. Wayne had no idea who lived there, or what he was looking for exactly.

Wayne walked to the front door and was about to ring the bell when suddenly the door flew open. Startled, he took a step back.

A beautiful young woman in her late teens, with long, wavy hair and soulful eyes, stood there. She looked nervous and sad.

"I'm Calia," she said before Wayne could say anything. "Len called and told us you would be coming over. Please come in."

Wayne was both pleased and surprised that Len had informed them. He obviously knew who lived here and wanted to prepare them for the visit.

"Thank you," said Wayne, following the lovely young woman into a large, open room with big windows that looked out over a lush garden.

"Len said you were coming to talk to us," Calia continued. "I'm so glad you are, we're all worried to death."

"About what?" Wayne was utterly fascinated.

"My father hasn't been home for over a week and we're worried," she exclaimed.

"Your father?" Wayne froze on the spot.

"Yes, my father, Mort Townsend," she said breathlessly. "Where is he? Len said you knew."

"Mort Townsend is your father?" Wayne could barely speak.

"Yes, of course. Is something wrong? You're frightening me. Tell me, please," begged Calia.

Wayne's head began spinning. "Who else lives here?" he managed to ask.

Calia didn't take his hesitation well. "My mother and my brother, Nate," she replied. "Tell me, where's my father?"

"Let's sit down a minute," Wayne said then, as gently as he could. "Is your mother home now, or your brother?"

"Yes, they both are." Calia's fear began to intensify.

"Can you ask your mother and brother to join us?" Wayne said then. He didn't want to tell Calia the news while she was alone.

"Mom," Calia called out loudly. "Come here right now. That person has come that Len mentioned."

"Okay, okay," Wayne heard a woman's voice calling back. "I'll be there in a minute."

"How about your brother?" Wayne asked.

"He's in his room. We don't like bothering him when he's busy," Calia replied.

Wayne nodded slowly, as a lithe, lovely, blonde woman in her late forties entered the room quickly.

"Who are you? Why are you here?" She stared at Wayne hesitantly.

"I'm Detective Wayne Darrington," he replied.

The woman looked stunned. "Why are we being visited by a detective?"

"Sit down, please," Wayne said gently, "and let's talk."

CHAPTER FOURTEEN

"I still don't understand why we're being visited by a detective," the woman repeated after they all sat down on a pair of velvet settees.

"Thank you for allowing me into your home," said Wayne, trying to create an atmosphere of at least temporary normality.

"Your daughter, Calia, just told me that Mort Townsend is her father," Wayne started off.

The woman trembled a moment and then stared at Wayne intensely. "Yes, that's right, and I'm Mort's wife, Heidi Townsend. I haven't heard from Mort for several days. Where is he?"

"Does this happen often?" Wayne asked. "Is it usual for Mort to stay away for a few more days?"

"Mort is a busy man," Heidi snapped at him. "He travels a lot. Of course, sometimes he stays a little longer than expected."

A long pause surrounded the three of them.

"But why has a detective come to my home now?" Heidi's eyes flashed open. "Has he gotten in trouble?"

"What kind of trouble would he get into?" asked Wayne, nervously.

"Let's just stop this game of ping-pong." Heidi flung her head back. "Answer me straight. Where is Mort? What's going on?"

Wayne couldn't bring himself to tell them yet. It would be too sudden. "What kind of trouble could Mort possibly be in?" he repeated.

Suddenly Heidi turned pale. "Mort's come to harm, hasn't he?" Her voice rose.

Calia lashed out instantly. "Why do you always think the worse, Mom? I'm sure Dad's just busier than usual this time around. Obviously, he didn't have time to contact us. So he's sending a message through the detective."

"Dad didn't have time?" Heidi's face distorted. "That's ridiculous. How long does it take to make a call? This is not like him. He doesn't send messages to me through other people."

Calia suddenly looked alarmed. "No it's not like him," she agreed.

Wayne knew he had to take control of what he felt was an oncoming storm. He couldn't hold back any longer.

"You're right," Wayne said then slowly. "Mort did not send me with a message, exactly."

"Well, I'm glad I'm right about something," snapped Heidi.

"May I talk to you openly in front of your daughter?" Wayne asked then.

"Of course, I'm not a child, I'm eighteen," Calia responded intensely.

"Say what you have to, right now!" Heidi consented.

"Actually, Mort did come to harm," Wayne spoke as carefully as he could.

"Harm? What happened?" Calia began trembling.

"Your father was found murdered on the beach in Key Biscayne a few days ago." Wayne looked at her carefully.

"What?" Calia looked as if she would faint. "Murdered? A few days ago?" She grabbed onto the edge of the settee. "Is this is a bad joke?"

"I'm really, really sorry," said Wayne, wishing he could do something to ease the pain.

"Murdered?" Heidi's voice rose, and she looked at Wayne as if he'd done it himself. "How do you know that?"

"How do I know that he was murdered?" asked Wayne.

"Yes," Heidi hissed furiously. "He could have had a terrible accident, couldn't he? Or for all we know he could have gone off the deep end and harmed himself."

"Dad would never harm himself," Calia yelled shrilly.

"What happened exactly, tell me!" Heidi insisted.

Wayne was reluctant to give them all the details at the moment. It would be too much to absorb all at once. As it was, Calia seemed completely uncomprehending and frozen.

"Dad had clinics he worked at in Key Biscayne," Calia said slowly, trying to put the pieces together. "He was there every week for half a week or so. Then he'd come home to us. He always said he was so happy to be here. We made him so happy."

"Yes, you did. I'm sure of it," said Wayne.

"Why didn't you inform us immediately?" Heidi's voice got louder. "Mort's been gone several days by now."

Wayne barely knew how to answer. "We didn't know about you," he finally said.

"Didn't know about us? What are you talking about?" Heidi grew unnerved.

"Of course we had the information about Mort's clinics in Nashville, but we didn't know that he had a second family." The words just came out on their own.

Heidi froze completely. "A second family? What are you talking about?"

Wayne closed his eyes and took a deep breath. Mort had been living a double life, each one completely separate from the other. How was it possible? Why did he do this? Wayne had no idea how to handle it. He was in way over his head.

"We're doing our best to find out all the details of Mort's life," Wayne said, circumventing the question.

"Answer me!" Heidi's voice rose sharply. "What do you mean a second family?"

"He doesn't know what he's talking about, Mom." Calia walked over to her. "He told us already that the police in Key Biscayne didn't even know about us. He doesn't either. They're imagining all kinds of crazy things."

"None of this makes sense." Heidi began wringing her hands.

Wayne saw a shadow at the side door then. He turned and saw a young man about seventeen, a little younger than Calia, standing there. He was slim and jumpy with rumpled hair.

"What's all the commotion?" the young man asked.

"What are you doing here, Nate?" Heidi zeroed in. "You have homework to do."

"This is my brother, Nate," Calia said in a low tone, as if she were trying to hold things together.

"Hello, Nate." Wayne took a step toward him.

"Who are you and what are you doing in my house?" Nate looked at Wayne suspiciously. "I've never seen you before."

"Nate is naturally nervous," said Heidi, rushing over to him. "I'll tell Nate the news myself slowly, later."

"Tell me what news?" Nate's eyes began squinting. "I'm not nervous. I'm just smarter than others."

"Dad is dead, he's gone," Calia burst out. "This man is a detective who came here to tell us that. Dad was found in Key Biscayne on the beach."

"We're not sure what happened, though," Heidi jumped in. "No one's positive yet."

"There's no reason to keep the truth from Nate, or pretend Dad's alive!" Calia wouldn't have it.

"Dead?" Nate came to a full stop. "I don't believe it!"

"It's true, it's true." Heidi suddenly began sobbing.

Nate ground his foot on the floor feverishly.

"Are you okay, Nate?" Wayne asked slowly.

"I'm not okay and I'm not surprised, either," Nate answered quickly. "I always told Mom and Calia that one day we'd all be like dead fish swimming in the ocean, doomed."

The heaviness and horror in the room intensified greatly. Wayne had to break into it; he decided to take action.

"I'm going to call the police in Key Biscayne now," he said. "They need to know about you."

"Then what?" Heidi spoke in a raspy tone, having trouble breathing.

"Then the police in Key Biscayne will be in immediate touch with the force here in Nashville," said Wayne. "The story will go out all over the local news so we can get clues to help find the killer."

"Our lives will be blasted all over the news?" Calia was beside herself. "What will they say about us?"

"We have to do it," said Wayne, somberly. "We need help finding the killer."

"The killer?" Nate echoed those words, as if tasting each one of them. "Why would the cops blast the news in Nashville if Dad was killed down in the Keys? That's where the police should be looking."

"They are," said Wayne, fascinated by Nate. He seemed to flip into different moods each moment.

Nate stared at Wayne strangely. "Are there any suspects yet? Even one who could have done it?"

Wayne felt chilled. Now Nate was suddenly so cool and calm.

"Not yet," said Wayne. "There are a few persons of possible interest, but nothing solid at all."

Nate shook his head swiftly. "Dumb ass cops," he said bitterly. "Soon it will be too late to find out who did it. Killers cover their tracks like poisonous snakes. The worst murders go cold in an instant."

"Yes, it's true," Wayne murmured, wondering how Nate knew all about it.

*

Wayne walked to the corner of the room and immediately called the police in Key Biscayne.

"Let me talk to Dowl," Wayne said the second someone picked up. "There's an emergency here."

Dowl got on immediately. "What's the emergency?" he asked hoarsely.

"Okay," Wayne breathed, "I've got big news for you. Sit down."

"Tell me what it is!" Dowl sounded nervous.

"Mort has a second family in Nashville. I'm in their home right now, talking to them."

A shocked silence greeted Wayne on the other end. "Are you crazy?"

"No, it's true," said Wayne.

"You're positive?" Dowl finally asked.

"I am," said Wayne. "We've got to spread the news of his death all over Nashville, and contact the cops here immediately."

"Absolutely," Dowl agreed. "We'll set up a call line for leads to come in from there, ASAP."

"I want Olivia up here working this with me now, too," Wayne continued.

"Certainly, she should fly right up," Dowl agreed. "What's going to happen, though, when the family in Key Biscayne finds out there's a second one in Nashville?"

"All hell's gonna break loose," Wayne responded. "And a lot more's about to come out. Get ready!"

"I'm ready," mumbled Dowl, half alarmed.

"The family up here's got a hell of a lot on their plate," Wayne continued. "They've got to deal with the father's death and also just found out that he has a second family."

"God." Dowl could barely take it all in. "I'm sure the police in Nashville are going to want to talk to all of them. They have to. The sooner the better, actually."

"I agree," said Wayne.

"And we're going to need to talk to them too," Dowl added. "Don't leave them alone right now. They've got to be reeling."

"No, I'm staying here for now," Wayne agreed.

"Do you want us to call Olivia for you and tell her to go up there?" Dowl asked.

"Absolutely not," said Wayne, irritated. "I have plenty of time to call her and tell her about this myself."

CHAPTER FIFTEEN

After Wayne helped Heidi make arrangements to have friends come over so she wouldn't be alone, he immediately put a call in to Olivia.

"How's it going?" Olivia asked as soon as she picked up. Olivia was pleased to finally hear from Wayne. He had been on her mind, strongly.

Wayne felt relieved to hear Olivia's voice, as well. "We've got an amazing development up here," he answered instantly.

"What? Tell me." Olivia was all ears.

Wayne jumped right in. "I just found out that Mort has a second family. In fact, I'm calling from their home."

"What are you talking about?" Olivia gasped.

"He has two wives and two sets of children," Wayne answered, still in disbelief himself. "One family lives here. The head administrator at Mort's clinic led me right to them."

Olivia could barely wrap her head around it. "You're positive this is true? Mort's been living a double life?"

"Exactly," said Wayne. "I want you to come up right away. The police will be talking to them shortly and I need you to be here when they do. Not only do I need your take on it, but it will also be good for the family to have you around. You'll calm things down. You always do."

"Absolutely." Olivia sounded shaken. "I'll take the first flight out this evening."

"Good," said Wayne. "I'll pick you up at the airport."

"Okay," Olivia agreed. She couldn't help thinking about Penny, Lance, and Christine, though. How in the world would they handle this insane turn of events? Their entire lives would be shaken to the core.

"This is going to be a nightmare for Mort's other family, as well," Olivia murmured.

"I know it is," said Wayne. "But somebody might have known something about this. For all we know this awful news will blow the rest of the case wide open."

"Okay, I'll text you when I have my flight information," said Olivia, eager to get going and make arrangements to be with Wayne.

Wayne put a call in to the police in Nashville then. Fortunately, by the time he called, Dowl had already spoken to them. And the chief of police in Nashville, Andy Pern, was ready and waiting to hear from Wayne.

"Good work, terrific!" Pern started.

"Thanks," said Wayne.

"People here know the Townsend family. If they need somebody to be with them, we'll be glad to send an officer over," Pern offered immediately.

"I believe Heidi has friends on their way over now," Wayne replied.

"Good," said Pern. "Okay, the news will be going out in a little while all over Nashville and the call line is almost ready."

Wayne took a deep breath. The family's life was about to totally change and there was nothing they could do about it. There was no way of knowing who would call in or what would turn up, either. It was one thing to lose someone you loved. It was another to find out that he was a totally different person, lived a double life you knew nothing about.

"We want to talk to Mort's family in the morning," Pern continued. "I hope you can be at the station with them."

"Of course," said Wayne. "I'll be there with my partner, Olivia."

"Perfect. It's a pleasure having you on board," Pern answered.

"It's a pleasure being here as well," said Wayne.

*

When Olivia arrived in Nashville, the first thing she saw was Wayne waiting at the landing gate. Excited to see her, he started waving.

"You got here in a minute," Wayne said, rushing to her.

"Two minutes, maybe?" Olivia smiled.

As they got closer, both reached out for the other, but stopped themselves at exactly the same time. They had agreed to keep the relationship entirely professional and were respecting their decision.

"I couldn't stop thinking of Mort's second family all during the flight," Olivia said as Wayne took her bag and guided her out of the airport.

"They're interesting people," said Wayne.

"They must be totally devastated," said Olivia. "To find out that he died and at the same time that he had a second family!"

"I can't even imagine," said Wayne, as he got a cab and they both jumped in. "You'll meet them tomorrow at the police station."

"The cast of characters widens," said Olivia, as she leaned near the window and the streets began to roll by. It was evening now and lights were on all over the city. "Jazzy town," she commented as they drove up to the hotel.

"I felt you'd love it here," said Wayne.

"You're right, I do," Olivia answered, impressed by what she saw. The town was beautiful, alive, rocking. It was a place she could be happy in, she thought.

"I've been so flummoxed by the second family, I'm afraid I've forgotten to ask you about what you've found so far," Wayne said then.

"There's nothing specific yet," Olivia replied. "I've just been getting a sense of the people in Mort's world. Justin's been talking to the same people as well."

Wayne stopped short. "Justin's been with you all this time?" He was startled.

"No, he's sort of shadowing me. He talks to people right after I do," said Olivia, noting Wayne's reaction.

"That's totally unnecessary." Wayne was miffed.

Olivia smiled to herself. Was Wayne threatened or maybe even jealous? Strangely enough, it made her feel good. Probably just a sense of professional pride, she thought. After all, what difference did it ultimately make if Justin was around or not?

"I guess the police feel the more eyes on a case the better," Olivia answered, putting Justin's presence into context.

Wayne turned to her, sad. "You're right, of course," he answered. "I just felt that maybe you suddenly had a new partner."

Olivia laughed. "You're the best work partner anyone could want, Wayne," she replied. "Nobody can replace you."

Wayne's face lit up.

"And, of course," she continued, "sooner or later, I'm definitely hoping a life partner will appear for me, as well."

"Of course," said Wayne, suddenly crestfallen.

"That person's definitely not Justin, though." Olivia wanted to ease Wayne's feelings.

"Thanks for saying that." Wayne reached out to her briefly, lightly putting his hand on hers. "It's a lot to handle all at once."

"Of course it is," said Olivia, giving his hand a squeeze. It must have been awful discovering a second family and having to bring them the horrible news of Mort's death.

In a few more moments Olivia and Wayne arrived at the hotel and checked in to their separate rooms. They agreed to meet early the next morning, first for breakfast and then to get to the police station.

Olivia went to her room, unpacked, and took a long bath. She could barely fall asleep though, kept tossing and turning. That was unusual for her and she wondered why. Of course, finding out that Mort had a second family was extremely unsettling. How had he kept the charade going? she wondered. And what was the need for such deceit? Was it possible that they were dealing with a man who had a split personality? Someone out there must have known the truth about him though, and hated him enough to put an end to his life.

It bothered Olivia that no one had caught any glimpse of Mort's deception before. There had to be someone who had some suspicions. Olivia looked forward to meeting the new family, seeing Mort's other side and what it said about him. She also suspected that more leads would come out when his family in Florida heard about this.

*

Right after breakfast, Olivia and Wayne made their way to the police station promptly. When they got there, Mort's Nashville family had already arrived. Olivia walked into the large waiting room and saw a beautiful teenage girl sitting on a wooden bench, crying. Beside her sat a stunning, fragile-looking blonde woman in her forties and next to her a tense young man.

Olivia immediately walked over to the family. "I'm Olivia Wells," she introduced herself. "Wayne and I work together. I am so very sorry for your loss."

The older woman's eyebrows rose, while the young girl looked at Olivia with gratitude.

"I'm Calia," she said softly. "Thanks for coming to help us. This is my mother, Heidi, and my brother, Nate."

"Why do you say thank you? How do you know Olivia's here to help us?" Nate grumbled under his breath.

"Of course I'm here to help you," Olivia responded, struck by his bitterness. "Wayne and I have been hired to find out who harmed your dad."

"Good luck." Nate scowled as a tall, lanky officer walked into the room.

The officer walked straight over to Wayne. "Wayne?" he asked. "Chief of Police Andy Pern."

"Yes, yes, hello," Wayne replied, shaking his hand. "This is my partner, Olivia Wells."

Andy Pern turned toward Olivia swiftly. "Glad to have you here to help," he replied. Then slowly he turned to the family. "We're so sorry for your loss," he said. "We really appreciate your coming in to help us so soon."

Heidi stood up shakily. "It's not so soon, though, I gather. From what I've discovered, my husband actually died several days ago."

Olivia felt startled to hear this woman call Mort her husband. Olivia could not help think of Christine.

Andy Pern shook his head. "We had no idea about your husband's death, really. Let's go inside my office and we'll talk more about it."

Everyone followed him into a more private room with softer chairs and a warmer feeling. Once everyone was seated, Calia began to cry.

"Tell us what you can about your father." Pern turned to Calia.

"He was a wonderful dad in every way," she replied. "I could count on him for everything."

Olivia watched Nate shift nervously as Calia spoke. "You too, Nate?" Olivia asked.

Nate shrugged sullenly. "Maybe," he remarked.

"I'm sure he was a great father, Calia," Pern said. "Do you have anything to add, Mrs. Townsend? Anything that might throw even the slightest light on what could have happened to your husband?"

Heidi looked like a bird caught in a storm. "No," she answered, "no idea at all. It's enough trying to make sense of what they're telling me, that Mort had another family. Is that true? Is it possible? I don't really believe it."

"It does look that way." Pern nodded his head somberly. "I can only imagine what a shock this has to be."

"Then I have nothing further to say." Heidi began to edge away. "Obviously, our whole life was a lie and I never even knew the person you're talking about, that ended up dead on the beach."

That was too much for Olivia. "No," she couldn't help but interject. "You knew part of your husband. The life Mort had with you and your family was real. There was just more to him that you knew nothing of."

To Olivia's surprise, Nate sneered.

"Do you agree, Nate?" asked Wayne. "Do you feel that you knew at least part of your father?"

"Of course I knew him," said Nate. "I knew everything about him, and so did my mom and sister."

"Everything?" asked Wayne, alarmed.

"When he was here, he was here. I knew who he was when he was here. A lot of time, he wasn't. We all got used to that."

"Was that hard for you?" Olivia couldn't help ask.

"It was that way since I was little," said Nate.

"You get used to things," Calia chimed in. "We never knew it to be any different."

"But that doesn't make it easy," said Olivia.

"Mort was not an easy man, ever," Heidi chimed in then. "He became more and more complicated, the longer we were married."

"You had a good marriage?" asked Olivia.

"I thought it was perfect, beautiful," said Heidi in a raspy tone. "He said over and over how happy I made him. He said nothing in the world ever made him so happy."

"That's beautiful," Olivia said, fascinated. "How did he get more complicated?"

"I don't know how to put it exactly," said Heidi. "Mort grew quieter, sometimes distant. Once he decided something, whatever you said, you couldn't budge him. I used to ask him if something was bothering him, but it only upset him. He said you're bothering me when you ask that question. Take me as I am."

"I'm sorry," said Olivia.

"Sometimes I felt it was something about me that disturbed him," Heidi went on. "At times I felt as though I was failing."

"There's nothing about you that could possibly upset him, Mom," Calia broke in, trembling. "People need quiet times, it's natural."

Nate sneered once again. "Nothing's natural about it," he muttered.

"What do you mean?" asked Wayne.

"I don't know what I mean." Nate shot Wayne a dark glance. "But nothing's natural here, is it?"

"Nate's a nervous young man and always has been," his mother quickly defended him. "You can imagine how awful it is for him to lose his father."

"Of course I can," replied Wayne.

Olivia found it fascinating to see these different aspects of Mort and his families. Nate may have been nervous and upset, but he also seemed exceptionally intelligent and perceptive for such a young man.

"Did Mort have friends in Nashville?" Wayne turned to Heidi then.

"Some, of course," said Heidi. "We had a few couples we went out with routinely. Mort wasn't a man who wanted a lot of company. He always said his family was more than enough for him. He loved us, or so I thought, anyway."

"Dad loved us, Mom. Of course he loved us," said Calia.

"Do you work as well?" Officer Pern asked Heidi.

"I worked in the music business in the beginning of the marriage, but pretty soon, I didn't have to. Mort's clinics did so well, he wanted me to stop working so he could pamper me. It was also very important to him that I stay at home to be here full time for the children."

"How did you spend your time when he was away traveling?" asked Olivia. "He was gone a lot."

Heidi shrugged nonchalantly. "I have friends of my own, naturally. And, of course, I cared for our family. Once in a while I arranged for local concerts, despite Mort's objections."

Olivia wasn't sure what the problem was with that. "What did he object to?"

Heidi smiled wanly. "Nothing, really, Mort just wanted all my attention focused on him. He didn't like anything taking me away from him, especially as he was only here part time."

Heidi was very well put together, and remarkably composed, thought Olivia. She probably was in shock, hadn't realized fully yet what happened. Finding out about Mort's other family could also be absorbing her attention, taking the edge off the reality that Mort was gone.

"Did you go down to Key Biscayne with Mort?" Pern asked Heidi then.

"No, I've never been down there," Heidi commented. "I like it here, and Mort never suggested that I accompany him during his work time. When we traveled together we went to Europe and spent all our time in galleries and museums. That was fine with me. It was plenty."

"I was never in Florida either," Nate suddenly chimed in, looking more and more bewildered. "I told my dad I wanted to go but he always said there was no reason for it. I said you don't need a reason for everything, do you?"

For a moment they all stared at each other.

"What did he say?" asked Wayne then.

"He said he'd take me to Florida when I got older. My father said lots of things that will never come true now, will they?" asked Nate.

Heidi stood up and brushed Nate's hair off his forehead. "You can't think that way," she said nervously. "Life will go on. We'll be all right. Dad would have wanted us to be happy. And who knows if he really had a second family, or someone has made all this up? People lie, Nate!"

"Don't I know it!" Nate shrugged oddly.

"You'll all have to go to Key Biscayne shortly," Chief Pern interjected, "and speak to the police there yourselves."

"Will we also meet the other family?" Nate perked up.

Pern and Wayne exchanged quick glances. "I believe that's important," said Wayne carefully. "Don't you?"

"Absolutely." Nate's voice got louder and shrill. "I want to see them with my own eyes. Do I have other brothers and sisters?"

"Seems so," Olivia said. "Two half brothers and a half sister. How about you?" Olivia turned to Calia.

"I don't know what's going on," Calia said sadly. "I can't believe it's true."

"We'll go down and find out," Nate insisted. "We'll all sit together in a room and talk. Don't you want to meet our other brothers and sister?"

At that Calia trembled violently. "No, I don't," she breathed. "No, no, no."

"I'm not sure this is a good idea at all," Heidi chimed in then. "I'm not sure I want to attend this meeting."

"It'll all be fine," Olivia assured her. She knew the police in Key Biscayne wanted them all to come down and that they had to. It would also be tremendously valuable for them to meet the other family. Once they did, all together, they would begin to be able to untangle the web of confusion and lies that Mort lived in.

CHAPTER SIXTEEN

Olivia and Wayne sat together stiffly on their flight back down to Key Biscayne, going over whatever they could find on their computers about Mort's second family. For now, nothing seemed out of order. Calia's social media pages were filled with friends and warm support for everything in her life, including her love of gymnastics and the many medals she'd won at it. Heidi seemed to be a bit more private, but as she said, she had a small group of loyal friends whom she clearly could count on. Nate's pages were sparser. He seemed to enjoy going on hunting expeditions and collecting guns.

"We're not going to find the answer on social media," Wayne commented halfway through the flight. "It will be the meeting in person between both families, down in Key Biscayne, that will open new doors."

"I don't know which will be harder for the families, to deal with their father's death, or the fact that he lived a secret life," Olivia mused.

"No matter how you cut it, Mort was a scoundrel," Wayne interjected. "Who does something like this?"

"He must have been torn apart inside," Olivia commented. "He obviously loved all of them."

"Nothing obvious about that," Wayne said. "This could have had nothing to do with love at all. Who knows what kind of pleasure he got out of playing these games, deceiving everybody?"

Olivia couldn't help but think of Todd once again. Had he also gotten pleasure out of sleeping with his former girlfriend just as he and Olivia were getting engaged? Was that also a game for him?

Olivia had never thought of it that way before. But it was true, and Mort could also have received a warped form of pleasure from living a double life. Having a secret like this could have made him feel powerful. Or, possibly, he had become mentally ill? Did he need two different lives to make him feel whole? Olivia wanted to speak to a psychologist about this.

The flight went quickly and as soon as they landed in Key Biscayne, Olivia and Wayne headed straight to the police station. Mort's family from Nashville had taken an earlier flight and most likely would be there already. Olivia felt uneasy about being at the meeting between them. For a second, she wished she could take hold of Wayne's hand or at least have his arm around her. Suddenly she felt alone in a world where nothing could be counted on.

Olivia stopped walking and stood there silently for a moment.

Wayne turned to her quickly. "Are you all right?"

"I'm not," said Olivia. "Actually, I'm feeling totally stranded now."

"Stranded? You're not. I'm right here." Wayne threw his arm around her shoulder, pulled her to him, and then gave her a quick hug.

The hug felt good, brief though it was. "I feel funny anyway," said Olivia, wishing they could remain closer.

"You're just feeling uncomfortable because we're about to see all of them meet each other. Nerve-wracking for sure."

*

When Olivia and Wayne got to the police station the main interrogation room was crowded. Both families had just arrived. Each family was standing on opposite sides of the room, gazing at one another fitfully. Both Angie and Andrea were also present. Olivia could understand why Angie would be there, but seeing Andrea there surprised her.

"Have any of you ever met?" Chief Dowl had taken charge and was running the meeting.

"Never, ever, ever." Christine waved her arms wildly over her head. "And I don't believe a word of this. They're lying, all of them."

Heidi stood a bit behind Calia, staring at Mort's flamboyant other wife.

Officer Dowl turned to the other members of the family and asked each the same question. Had any of them ever seen each other before? One by one they all denied it.

"These are not my husband's children," Christine burst out again, pointing to Calia and Nate. "I officially deny this insane story."

Calia took great exception to that. "Deny it all you want." Her voice now suddenly became authoritative. "There are many people in Nashville who can confirm it. We've lived there as a family for years."

"Are there documents to prove this?" Lance asked Dowl then, in a balanced tone. "Are there marriage certificates and certificates of birth?"

Somehow Lance's question upset Andrea. "What difference does that make?" she interjected. "Something written on a piece of paper doesn't really make someone a husband or father."

"What are you talking about?" Calia shuddered. "Who are you anyway?"

"I'm Andrea, a part of the family, and I'm saying that someone can be a great father to you, even if he's not your father legally."

"Maybe," Calia uttered, "but Mort Townsend was my natural birth father!"

"Don't even bother to fight with her, honey," Heidi whispered to her daughter. "Obviously, she's delusional. Who knows who these people really are?"

Angie raised his hand forcefully then, to calm everyone down. "Let's not get sidetracked here," he insisted. "Of course we need legal documents to see who's who and what's what. There's lot of money at stake in Mort's inheritance."

"Is that what you're concerned with? Only that?" Heidi's eyes shot fire at him.

"I'm concerned with much more than that," Angie answered, "but that's a part of it as well."

"Bigamy is not permitted in our nation," Lance informed them calmly. "Only one wife here is the legal one. Only one family receives my father's inheritance."

Heidi stared at Olivia unbelievingly. "That's all they're concerned with! Money, money," she breathed.

"A great deal depends upon when you and Mort married," Lance continued. "And from the look of it, from the age of the children, it seems my mother was his first wife."

"Which means you are not even Mort's wife," Christine said loudly. "You're simply a mistress of some sort."

"She's insulting you, Mom," Calia retorted. "Don't pay any attention to what she says."

"Heidi is not a mistress." Penny tried to calm the waters. "It's possible that all along she's believed that she's Dad's wife. Don't rip everything away from her at once, Mom. We have to sort out this confusion slowly."

"What am I ripping? I'm just speaking the truth," exclaimed Christine.

"My mother is definitely Mort Townsend's wife and I am his daughter," Calia insisted.

"According to who? Only to you!" Andrea shot back at them, as though she were in charge of the meeting.

"Shut the hell up." Nate lunged toward Andrea.

"Who are you to talk to me that way?" Andrea snapped back.

"Calm down, Andrea." Penny tried to stop her. "Andrea's my best friend," she explained to Calia. "She's been like a sister since we met."

"That counts for nothing," Nate murmured, his face growing distorted.

"I am not like a sister, I *am* Penny's sister," insisted Andrea. "And even though I'm not a sister by birth, I'm better than most sisters she could have."

Penny put her hand on Andrea's shoulder. "It's all right," she told her.

"No, it isn't." Andrea shook her hand off. "All of a sudden people have arrived from out of nowhere, claiming to be Mort's children. It more than I can bear."

"Claiming?" Nate's eyes narrowed as he practically lunged at her again.

"Calm down, Andrea." Lance was now growing uneasy. "This will all be checked into thoroughly, to see when and if marriage certificates were filed. From my research so far I do see that Morton A. Townsend, our father as we know him, filed a marriage certificate with my mother. I've also noted a Morton J. Townsend filing a marriage certificate in Nashville. We have to check further to make sure that's the father of Nate and Calia, and that he's the same man."

"Of course he is." Nate let loose.

"Shut up, Nate. Shut up." Andrea glared at him.

"Let Andrea say what she wants." Christine now seemed to be enjoying this. "She's not a daughter, but she is a good friend of the family, definitely!"

Christine's comment only incensed Andrea further, however. "Who can say who is and isn't family?" Andrea shot back.

"Seems you're the most upset about meeting Mort's second family." Dowl turned to Andrea then.

"It's not that," Andrea breathed, "I just hate it when people act as if everyone has a father but me."

"Maybe you don't deserve one," Nate hissed at her.

Startled by Andrea's behavior, Olivia jumped in. "You had absolutely no idea about Mort's second family?" she asked her.

"Of course not, how could I?" Andrea answered. "Even though I worked closely with Mort, he never mentioned them, ever. Not a word. To anybody."

"How closely did you work with Mort?" Olivia pursued it.

"Very," Andrea said, boldly claiming her place. "We interacted every single day. Even when he was in Nashville."

"Have you ever been there?" Dowl jumped into the conversation now.

"Yes, I was actually," Andrea responded, "two or three times only, though."

Everyone looked at Andrea differently then.

"Why?" asked Dowl, uneasy.

"Business, of course," Andrea quipped.

"Do the people at Mort's clinics in Nashville know you?"

"Some might remember me, I have no idea," said Andrea.

Dowl threw a strange glance over at Wayne then. "We'll look into this," he said.

"I'll check this out with Len Radson," Wayne commented.

"I don't know Len Radson," Andrea spoke loudly. "I did other things up there."

"What?" asked Dowl.

"Other things," said Andrea, "all just business."

"Monkey business," Nate chimed in.

"You have no choice but to tell us exactly what you did," Dowl continued.

"I looked over one or two of the clinics that Mort had some questions about," Andrea reported. "There were some questions about the medical assistants and Mort wanted me to check on it."

"You have proof of that?" Nate suddenly shouted.

"What's it to you?" Andrea spun around.

"It's my dad who was killed, not your dad," Nate yelled.

"And maybe he deserved what he got," Andrea suddenly spit out, growing more flushed and agitated.

"Maybe he did." Nate suddenly laughed.

Everyone stopped cold then and stared at both Nate and Andrea.

Dowl raised his hands. "Okay, okay, enough of this for now. The general meeting is over. We're going to want to talk to each of you separately in a little while. But first Nate and Andrea."

It was obvious to Olivia that right on the spot, both Andrea and Nate had turned into suspects. Olivia felt deeply unsettled. The meeting was far from over for her. Dowl could talk to Andrea and Nate alone all he wanted, but she personally wanted to interview both Christine and Heidi in a room together. The meeting between the two wives would be pivotal. Olivia could not help but feel that she would learn much of what she needed to know by watching them interact with each other.

"Before we adjourn the meeting I'd like to speak alone with Christine and Heidi together now," Olivia piped up.

"Terrific idea," Wayne agreed, looking at Olivia with interest.

Olivia quickly turned to Dowl. "How about it?"

"Of course, go right ahead," he replied. "The second room to the right is empty. The three of you can go there now. Stay as long as you like."

*

Olivia, Christine, and Heidi stood facing one another in a small room with a high window through which rays of sun managed to shine in. As soon as Olivia closed the door behind them, she pointed to narrow wooden chairs that were placed around a square table.

"Please sit down," Olivia suggested.

"These lousy chairs won't hold me. I'd rather stand," Christine said in a rough tone as Heidi went to sit as requested. Today Heidi seemed even more frail and unhinged as she placed her beautifully manicured hands on the table. She kept tapping her fingers together again and again.

Christine, though, seemed stronger, as though somehow Mort's death had given her an odd power and the right to dominate everyone. Christine looked at Heidi with scorn.

"I was married to Mort longer than you. Our children are older," she said.

Heidi did not answer, just looked over at Olivia, in pain. "I miss him terribly," she managed, somehow strangely suggesting that Christine did not.

"Do you miss him, too, Christine?" Olivia asked.

"I did terribly until today when I have to meet his so-called second family," Christine uttered.

"The thought of not seeing Mort again is not bearable," Heidi continued. "I don't care who I do or do not have to meet."

Christine's face grew red and hot. "I can't listen to this," she burst out. "Another woman is sitting here telling me she misses my husband. Another woman has memories with him. How can I live with this? I can't. He deceived both of us!"

Suddenly, the two of them stared at each other as if two flaming arrows shot in different directions had suddenly met and collided midstream.

"There had to be some sign that Mort lived a double life," Olivia uttered. "A person can't go on like this for years without

98

exposing it somehow. Mort must have wanted to expose it! He must have needed to tell the truth!"

"What makes you think he didn't tell the truth?" Christine's voice boomed out. "What makes you think the little side trip he had in Nashville meant anything to him at all?"

"Little side trip?" Heidi seemed totally offended.

"Heidi had to be something to pass the time while he was away from us." Christine breathed heavily.

"Just pass the time, for almost twenty years?" Heidi flared up. "There had to be something wrong in your relationship and you know it. He might have met me after he knew you, but he never left me. And he couldn't leave you obviously, even if he wanted to."

"Mort was brutally beaten," Christine flung back, wanting to see Heidi squirm. "He died a terrible death."

Heidi remained calm, though, seeming only to want to block Christine out.

"I'd hoped the two of you would join together to help us find Mort's killer," Olivia said then out of nowhere. "Someone knows something that can unlock the case."

The two women stopped and looked at one another. They couldn't have been more different, thought Olivia. They probably represented two completely different sides of Mort and what he needed.

"It seems to me that Mort could have possibly been quite ill mentally?" Olivia started probing.

Christine laughed loudly at the suggestion, while Heidi clenched up tighter.

"Mort was clear, simple, loyal," Heidi said. "He never showed any signs of mental illness at all."

"Living a total lie is mental illness." Christine seemed happy to say it.

"Yes, it is," agreed Olivia. "How else did he express this illness?" She turned to Christine.

"What illness? What are you talking about?" Heidi stood up from her seat then, frazzled. "I refuse to listen to this kind of nonsense. Say what you want about him, but Mort was not mentally ill. He was a fantastic businessman, smart and kind. Respect the dead, please. He deserves that much at least."

Christine's eyes narrowed painfully. "I did respect him, I used to respect him." She crouched over as she spoke. "But now I don't. How can I? Mort lied to me! He lied to you!"

"He must have gotten caught in a trap he couldn't get out of." Heidi began crying. "He got in over his head. We've all done that, and then we're sorry."

"Making excuses for him?" Christine laughed. "I used to do that too, in the beginning."

"What did you make excuses about, Christine?" Olivia jumped in.

"Every little thing he did that upset me," she said.

"Like what?" Olivia needed to know.

"Nothing so important, not something like this." Christine backed off promptly.

"But what?" Olivia wouldn't let go.

"He wouldn't come home at night when he said he would. I'd be there waiting with dinner," Christine murmured.

"Me, too, me too," Heidi echoed.

"I'd tell myself it was fine, he was working so hard for us," said Christine.

"You didn't press him about where he was?" Olivia was fascinated.

"Sometimes I did," Christine agreed, "but it just backfired. Mort was not a man who liked to be pressed. So I let it go and moved along."

Heidi was staring at Christine, mesmerized.

"As time went on it became a pattern," Christine continued. "I didn't press him. I didn't look deeply. Recently he wasn't bringing home as much money. I asked him where it was going and he looked at me blankly."

Heidi sighed deeply. "Oh my God, my God," she whimpered.

"You too?" Christine faced her head on.

"Exactly, exactly," said Heidi.

"Obviously, some other financial need has arisen for him. This would explain the money that was unaccounted for at his company," said Olivia.

"What are you talking about?" Christine grew rabid suddenly. "What unaccounted-for money?"

"Mort had a personal bank account through the company," Olivia reported. "Taxes were paid on it fully, but where the money went was unaccounted for."

"There could be another one of us! Another woman?" Heidi's head flipped backward in horror. "There was less money for our family as well."

Christine closed her eyes tight and stomped her foot on the floor. "He's lucky he's dead right now, I can tell you. Or I would have killed him myself if he was alive and I found all this out."

CHAPTER SEVENTEEN

Olivia spoke with Christine and Heidi a few minutes longer and then decided to give everyone a much needed break.

"Is this all there is?" Heidi asked disconsolately as Olivia said they would be stopping now.

"No, of course not," said Olivia, "we'll talk more later. There are other things I have to check on now."

"Like what?" Christine turned to Olivia suspiciously.

"I want to see what calls are coming in on the tip line, for one." Olivia wanted to be as transparent as possible. "I'm also interested in speaking to Nate."

At that Heidi shivered. "Why Nate?"

"He interests me," said Olivia.

"He's just a young boy, he's just lost his father." Heidi took exception.

"I'll be careful with him," Olivia assured her.

"I thought Dowl wanted to talk to him and Andrea," Christine interrupted.

"Yes, he does," agreed Olivia. "But I do, too."

Christine and Olivia looked at one another harshly. "You're pretty aggressive, really," Christine suddenly said to Olivia. "You look so mild and pretty, but that's not it at all."

Olivia wondered why Christine was turning on her now. "No, you're right, I'm not the least bit mild," Olivia retorted.

"Well, I'm glad you admit it at least," Christine added.

"What's the point of attacking me, if I may ask?" Olivia went on.

"I'm not attacking you, I'm not attacking anyone," Christine muttered. "I just want to keep things straight. Call something what it is. I've had it with being tricked and deceived."

"Why in the world would I want to deceive you?" asked Olivia.

Christine looked at her oddly then and smiled. "There are a lot of people here besides Nate who could be hiding something. Why aren't you talking to them? Why are you picking on a kid and the grieving widow?"

Christine's comment unnerved Olivia. Her suspicions of Olivia were totally unwarranted and they led Olivia to wonder what Christine was hiding herself.

"I don't like your talking to Nate either," Heidi chimed in sadly.

Olivia had enough. "Well, whether you like it or not, there's no choice about it. This is a murder investigation and that's exactly what I'm going to do."

*

After Christine and Heidi left, Olivia immediately texted Dowl that she wanted to speak to Nate as soon as he was available. To her delight, Dowl texted back instantly.

Nate's waiting outside. I haven't talked to him yet, I'm busy with Andrea. She's a piece of work. You go ahead. Wayne is talking to Lance, and, by the way, Justin is here, too, talking to some of the other folks now.

Olivia was surprised. What was Justin doing here, and how would Wayne react to that? She went out to the waiting area, where Nate was fidgeting on a small bench.

"Nate," Olivia said, "I'd really love to talk to you."

"About what?" Nate perked up instantly.

"About anything you'd like to talk about." Olivia tried to befriend him.

Nate seemed to like her and was game. "Sure," he said, gathering his backpack. "It's about time I talked to someone."

Olivia was pleased to hear that. "Great, let's go," she said as she guided Nate to the empty room where Christine and Heidi had just been sitting. Olivia felt uneasy about her time with both of the women. She instinctively felt it would be much better talking to Nate now.

"How are you holding up, Nate?" Olivia asked.

"I've been better," he said. "How about you?" Nate looked tired and lonely, with his long brown hair hanging down on his forehead. He was definitely unusual, but there was also something endearing about him.

Olivia smiled at him. "I'm doing fine, thanks for asking," she said.

"Seems like you had a rough time before with Andrea," Olivia commented as they settled down.

"Andrea's definitely creepy," Nate responded. "But at least she's not in the family, really, and I'll never have to see her again."

103

"Did Andrea give you a hard time?" Olivia kept on it.

Nate shook his head. "No one actually gives me a hard time."

"Really? How come?" Olivia found him fascinating.

"Because," Nate answered brusquely, "I'm on top of things. I see what's in front of my nose. I always did and always will."

"What do you see about this situation, Nate?" Olivia became conspiratorial, as if it were just the two of them against the world.

"I see that my mom's in big trouble." Nate scowled.

"Your mom?" Olivia was startled by his response.

"Yeah, she's just lost her husband, hasn't she?" He looked at Olivia oddly. "And she's not the strongest tree in the woods."

"Yes, of course, I see what you mean," Olivia replied.

"No, you don't. You don't really see. No one here does," he answered.

"I'm trying." Olivia smiled.

Unexpectedly, Nate smiled back. "I know you're trying," he said, "and that's why I like you."

"Why, thank you." Olivia was touched.

"You don't know what to do next though, do you?" Nate said then.

Nate threw Olivia off balance. "It's confusing, for sure," she admitted. "Any suggestions?"

Nate seemed to like being talked to like an adult, as if he had something valuable to contribute. But suddenly, he pulled back. "I don't have any ideas," he said, clamming up.

"What was your parents' marriage like?" Olivia tried a new tack with him.

"How do I know, really? It wasn't my business," he answered abruptly.

"Were they happy?" Olivia bypassed his objection.

"How does anyone know who is or isn't happy?" Nate grew disturbed.

"Are you hiding something from me, Nate?" Olivia pulled her chair a bit closer.

"Maybe? I have a right to hide things, don't I?" He suddenly looked strangely at her.

"Not when there's a murder investigation going on," Olivia answered softly.

"But if the person who was murdered was my father, I have a right!" Nate insisted. "I'm a victim too, aren't I?"

"Why would you want to hide things, though?" Olivia was all over it. "Don't you want to help us find the killer?"

"Maybe I do and maybe I don't," Nate replied, confusing Olivia further.

"You were close to your dad?" She dove in further.

"At times we were close, other times we weren't," Nate answered crisply.

"Nate, you're hiding something, and I feel it," Olivia responded. "Please tell me! You're not glad that your father is gone, are you?"

At that Nate stood up boldly. "That's a dumb, stupid question."

"Answer it," Olivia demanded.

"I wouldn't say I'm glad exactly," Nate finally burst out. "But I'm not stupid either. I knew all along he had another life."

Olivia was astonished. "You knew?" She could barely breathe. "How did you know?"

"I told you I'm not stupid," Nate repeated. "I always wondered about him. Then, one day I found the secret photo album that my father kept under his bureau. His gig was up!"

"Did he know that you found it?"

"No," said Nate. "Why would I give that away? I wanted to see all the pictures he added to it, know how things were going. I had to know what was in store for us, didn't I?"

"Do you know where that album is now?" Olivia asked tentatively.

"I have it!" Nate's eyes gleamed. "Where else would it be? I even brought it down here with me when we came to Florida."

"It's in your room at the hotel?" Olivia felt breathless.

"Yup. I brought it because I knew it would be important in finding the real killer," Nate added.

"Does your mother know about it? Does Calia?"

"Nobody knows but you and me," Nate whispered.

"Nate, will you show it to me?" Olivia was on pins and needles.

Nate paused a long time and looked at her closely. "I will," he said finally. "I have to go back to my room and get it."

"Oh my God," Olivia breathed. "I'll get someone to go with you."

"Fine," Nate agreed. "We can look at it together then. In fact, why don't you come over to my hotel with me you're finished here. We'll go someplace secret and open it up. I'll wait and we can go together."

"Good idea," said Olivia, "perfect. Let me call Chief Dowl and see if I can leave the station now."

Olivia put a call in to Dowl immediately. "Can I go back to Nate's hotel with him now?" she asked. "He has something in his possession that might be crucial."

"What?" asked Dowl, startled.

"I'll tell you all about it after I see for myself," said Olivia.

"Sure, you can go there with him, but not this second," Dowl replied. "In fact, I was just going to call you. I've gotten new information from Andrea and I'd like you and Wayne to join the interrogation right now, to see what you think."

The case was beginning to spin like a whirling top, thought Olivia. "Of course," she replied. "I'll have Nate wait for me here."

"Good," said Dowl, "come right in now and join us."

*

When Olivia entered the interrogation room, Wayne was already there, seated a few feet away from Andrea. He waved Olivia in and pointed to a seat near him.

"Glad you're here," he said.

"Of course," said Olivia. "Fill me in."

"Maybe we should let Andrea fill you in herself," Wayne suggested, looking right at her.

Andrea shrugged. "I talked to Olivia already," she said.

"Really?" Dowl was surprised.

"We spoke briefly," Olivia recalled. "Andrea told me about her relationship with Penny, that they were like sisters. And that she worked for Mort."

"I also told you I never had a father," Andrea continued, bitterly. "Seems everybody has a father but me."

"Yes, I recall," said Olivia, deciding not to mention that many people didn't have fathers, or had fathers they didn't like very much.

Andrea spun around toward her. "And I also told you that I didn't like Mort that much. Remember?"

Olivia did remember. "Yes," she said, "it troubled me."

"Right, and so now everyone else is also troubled," Andrea continued, "because I also told them something else."

"What?" asked Olivia nervously.

Andrea's face grew taut as she looked over at Wayne.

"Tell her everything," Wayne exclaimed. "We need all eyes on the case."

Andrea looked away, though, and grew quiet, not wanting to go on.

"Andrea told us that Mort made a pass at her," Wayne spoke for Andrea.

"Made a pass?" Olivia was surprised.

"Yes, he did." Andrea's voice grew edgy. "And then he got scared and paid me money not to say a word."

This was a whole different level. "Not to say a word to who?" Olivia was disturbed.

"Well, for starters, Mort knew I was very close to his daughter, Penny," Andrea said.

"Did you say anything about this to her?" Olivia looked askance.

"Of course not, why would I? And I didn't take his money, either. I asked him what kind of woman he thought I was. He grinned and said all women were the same kind of women."

"Do you have evidence of this?" Olivia was appalled.

"You, too, asking me for evidence?" Andrea began to look frazzled. "You, too, suspecting the victim, shaming her? I could understand why Wayne or Dowl would ask that, but you? Another woman?"

"Hold on, wait a minute." Olivia felt frightened. "I'm not shaming you. It's a reasonable request."

"You are shaming me!" Andrea bit her lip hard.

"What about his wife?" Wayne jumped in then. "You mentioned there was tension between the two of you."

"Of course there was tension! Why wouldn't there be?" Andrea insisted. "Christine was always jealous of me. She was jealous that I was so close to Penny. She didn't want another daughter in her home. And she was always letting me know that Mort belonged to her! Only her."

"Why would she have to let you know that?" Olivia felt rankled.

"She must have seen the way Mort looked at me. Others saw it too. Ask Margaret, the next door neighbor, if you like. She commented on it many times. She told me Mort was totally drawn to me, probably couldn't live without me."

That seemed farfetched to Olivia. "How would Margaret have known something like that?" Olivia didn't know what to believe here. Andrea already had developed a fantasy that she and Penny were sisters. Was it possible she was fantasizing about her relationship with Mort as well? Not only was it possible, it was likely, thought Olivia.

"Very often when Margaret would drop in to visit, I'd be there with Mort and Christine," Andrea went on. "Margaret saw what was going on and even mumbled about it a few times. I told her, don't worry, every dog has his day. He'll definitely get punished for this one day."

The room grew silent when Andrea said that.

"Punished how?" Dowl asked, his face getting tight.

"Punished, just punished," Andrea murmured. "No one gets away with everything scot-free. Some things, maybe, but not everything. Do they?"

Olivia took a ragged breath then. Andrea's comment startled her. It didn't sound good.

"Andrea told some of this to us earlier," Dowl went on, intensely. "I've actually asked Christine to come and join us, to see what she says about it all."

"How dare you? This is my private interview." Andrea was horrified.

"There's nothing private about a murder investigation," Dowl informed her. "A man is dead and we have to find out why and who."

*

Christine arrived in a few moments, looking more upbeat than before. She'd put on a gleaming beaded necklace of red and pink that she hadn't worn before.

"That's quite a necklace," Olivia mentioned as soon as Christine sat down.

"It's number one on my line." Christine ran her hand over it lightly. "Makes me feel better when I'm down."

Andrea stared at the necklace as well.

"Mrs. Townsend," Dowl started the interview off, "I regret having to bring up this matter, but we can't hold anything back."

"What matter? Ask me whatever you like." Christine was now in grand form, her voice loud and piping.

"It's come to our attention that your husband might have shown personal attention to other women that was inappropriate," Dowl went on carefully.

Christine simply threw her head back and laughed. "Ridiculous! Like who, exactly?"

"Like Andrea, perhaps. Andrea mentioned that your husband made a pass at her," Dowl continued.

At that Christine laughed louder. "Yes, yes, of course she thinks that. Andrea lives in a dream world of her own. She only wished he would make a pass at her, so she could steal him away from me."

Olivia felt dizzy listening to Christine speak. There was a hollowness in her tone that was nerve-wracking. Olivia looked over at Andrea, who seemed entirely untouched by Christine's comments.

"Andrea was always jealous of both Penny and myself," Christine continued. "I told Penny not to bring her around so much, but Penny refused to listen. Penny can be headstrong if she wants. I told her that Andrea was not part of our family, although she fancied herself to be."

Andrea stood up suddenly and glared at Christine. "Penny never said a word to me about this," she uttered. "She told me I was always welcome, and Mort said the same thing."

Christine scraped her throat violently. "Oh, please," she uttered. "Take a hint, why don't you? What else could they say? You threw yourself all over us! We couldn't get away!"

Andrea turned her back forcefully on Christine and walked to the other side of the room.

Wayne got up and followed her there.

"You don't have to follow me wherever I go," Andrea shouted at Wayne. "I can come and go as I please. I don't let wretches like Christine get to me."

"Look how bad-tempered she is, too." Christine took advantage of the outburst to attack Andrea further. "But don't worry, we'll get it all cleared up. My brother Angie is on his way here now with Margaret. Angie's been pinning people down, talking to everyone."

Olivia was delighted that Margaret would be here soon. It seemed she was an important part of the puzzle. They all wanted to hear what she had to say.

"For now, you both can go home," Dowl said to both Christine and Andrea. "We'll be in touch again shortly."

"And what if I don't want to?" Christine piped up.

"It's better this way for everyone," Wayne said to her kindly. "Olivia and I will let you know what happens."

"Yes, when this is over, call me immediately," Christine ordered, as she stood up grandly and swept out of the room.

After Christine left, Andrea walked out quietly, not looking at anyone or saying a word.

CHAPTER EIGHTEEN

After Andrea and Christine left, in almost no time at all, a loud knock sounded on the door.

"Open," Dowl called out. "Come in."

"Is Christine still here?" Angie boomed out as he entered with a wan, agitated, middle-aged woman.

"No, she just left," Wayne announced. "All clear."

"Okay, Margaret, see, I told you Christine would be gone when you got here," Angie said to the woman.

Margaret looked around the room hurriedly to make sure they were alone. "I don't know what I'm doing here." Her words tripped over one another. "I haven't done a thing, and I've never been to a police station before."

"Being here doesn't mean you've done anything wrong." Wayne stood up to greet her. "You're just here to help us understand Mort better."

"But I don't really want to be here," Margaret insisted.

"This is a murder investigation," Wayne said softly. "You have to tell us what you know."

"I must?" Margaret began to tremble a little.

Angie suddenly jumped in. "Margaret's an important witness! She told me that Andrea had a vendetta against Mort. Andrea mentioned it to her."

"What kind of vendetta?" Dowl's forehead creased. "That's a pretty serious accusation."

"I didn't mean a vendetta actually." Margaret immediately corrected Angie. "Mort just made Andrea uncomfortable, and me, too. Andrea and I talked about it once in a while."

"How did Mort make you uncomfortable?" Olivia was all over it.

Margaret spoke in hushed tones. "Mort was an odd guy, not exactly as he seemed. One night I saw him looking into my house through the bushes. He was staring right up into my bedroom on the second floor. I screamed, but no one heard me."

"He was a peeping Tom?" Wayne looked amazed.

"I don't know if he was a peeping Tom, but he was definitely looking right into my bedroom window," Margaret insisted. "Thank

God, I was dressed. I shut the light immediately and when I looked down there a little while later, he was gone."

"That's scary," Olivia empathized.

"Terrifying," Margaret agreed. "I couldn't sleep all night. I kept getting up and going to the window again and again to make sure he wasn't there."

"Did it happen more than one time?" Dowl questioned.

"No, just that once," said Margaret.

Dowl shook his head slowly. "Unlikely," he said. "Usually peeping Toms do it over and over."

Margaret took offense. "I never said Mort was a peeping Tom. I said one night I saw him do it. Who knows how many other times he did and I never noticed?"

"Anything else?" Dowl wasn't finding this very convincing.

"Well, Christine was definitely very jealous of Andrea," Margaret marched forward bravely. "Once when Mort and Andrea were in the backyard I heard Mort try to get Andrea to leave. He told her Christine would be home soon and he didn't want to upset her. But Andrea refused to go."

"You heard this firsthand?" Dowl looked at her closely.

"Absolutely," said Margaret, heating up now. "Another time when I heard Christine and Mort fighting she told him he'd better get Andrea out of their home, or else!"

"Or else what?" asked Wayne.

"Or else there would be hell to pay," Margaret uttered. "And Christine isn't the kind of woman to make statements in vain. But I couldn't really blame her, either. Andrea hung around too much. Once I told Andrea that she was there too often and she just guffawed. This is my home, she finally said. I was flabbergasted." Margaret suddenly looked exhausted. "That's all I have to say."

"That's a hell of a lot," said Dowl. "Are you saying we have some weird stalker on our hands?"

"You're putting words in my mouth." Margaret became agitated. "I never called Andrea a weird stalker, and I never called Mort a peeping Tom."

"This definitely implicates Andrea though, doesn't it?" Angie jumped in. It was easy to see how badly he wanted to take the pressure off Christine.

There was nothing definite about it, though, Olivia thought. In fact, based upon Margaret's statement, Christine seemed equally suspicious as well.

"Thanks very much for your time, Margaret." Dowl stepped forward. "This is valuable information. You've been a help."

That pleased Margaret very much. "Of course," she said, glancing at Angie and smiling. "I told Angie I would do whatever I could to help find the killer. I don't know how this helps, but I'm glad you think it did."

Margaret walked toward the door then and Angie followed close after her.

"I'm not stopping," Angie muttered, "until we've got all we need."

After Angie and Margaret left, Olivia, Wayne, and Dowl looked at each other, puzzled.

"There's possible motive here for both Andrea and Christine," Dowl started. "At the moment, Andrea looks worse to me."

"Agreed," said Wayne. "It definitely could be that Andrea's not completely in touch with reality."

"Who is?" Olivia couldn't help but remark.

Wayne looked at Olivia oddly.

"Of course, some are further out than others," Olivia corrected herself. "Could be Andrea really thought Mort was her father and when she realized he wasn't, it pushed her over the edge."

"A revenge killing?" Dowl mused.

"It's a possibility," Olivia suggested, "but Christine also has intensely changing moods. I found it odd that she put that necklace on suddenly."

"Nothing odd about it," Dowl disagreed. "Christine's trying to act as if things are normal. I've seen victims of loss behave this way plenty of times. Some never take the time to grieve, work things out, or get adjusted. They go on as if everything is the same and life hasn't dealt them a horrible blow."

For a moment Olivia wondered about herself. She, too, was a victim of a terrible loss when Todd had been murdered. She'd also plunged forward into a new life as a detective instantly. There had been one case after another, too. Olivia hadn't had the time to stop and be aware of the choices she was making and the effects Todd's death really had on her.

"Both women could look suspicious, for sure," Wayne weighed in. "But there's no hard evidence here yet. We need to get something definite before we can say we have a real person of interest."

"Absolutely," Olivia chimed in then. "And it may not be either of them. Let me go now, Nate's been waiting for me outside. There's something important he has to show me."

Wayne jumped up and walked over to Olivia. "We need time to talk alone, too," he said hurriedly. "It's been too long."

"I know," said Olivia. "We'll debrief after my meeting with Nate."

*

Nate was restless when Olivia walked over to the bench he'd been waiting at.

"You sure took plenty of time," he muttered.

"I'm so sorry, Nate," breathed Olivia. "There are lots of different witnesses being questioned."

Nate smirked. "I bet," he said under his breath. "These cops can dredge up anyone to make it look good for them."

Olivia got a cab quickly and she and Nate went back to his hotel.

"You wait for me down here," he said when they arrived. "I'll get the album and then we can go down to look at it on Ardon Lane. I like it there."

"Sure thing," said Olivia, getting out of the cab and waiting for Nate outside. His hotel was a long, wooden building near the beach. From where she stood, Olivia could watch the evening clouds come in and smell the salty ocean sir. She wondered where Ardon Lane was and how Nate had found it.

Olivia then thought about her time at the police station and was glad that Wayne had seemed so eager to speak to her alone. He was right, it had been a while since they'd had time to go over things privately. She missed it as well.

In a few minutes Nate came running out, holding a big bag with something stuffed in it. It had to be the photo album, thought Olivia.

"Let's walk this way," said Nate, turning to the right and saying nothing further as they walked down to the edge of the hotel and then turned down a hill, to a dirt road that ended near a clump of old trees, rocks, and sand.

"The place looks like a cemetery, doesn't it?" Nate asked, looking around.

It didn't really, and Olivia felt uneasy at Nate's remark.

"Sit down on the sand," said Nate, as he walked a few steps and planted himself on a tree stump. "Rain's coming tonight, but it's not here yet and the sand won't be damp."

Olivia sat down on the sand as Nate pulled the photo album out of the bag and grabbed it tightly to him. Just the idea of opening it up seemed to upset him and he started scowling again.

"It's hard to look at the pictures, isn't it?" Olivia remarked.

"No, it isn't," Nate shot back. "I actually like looking at them. The last few months my father became more and more distant. He hardly looked at me at all. I knew something awful was brewing. When I asked him about it, he just turned away. So I can look at him now all I like."

"What did you think was bothering your father?" Olivia was troubled.

"Just take a look at these photos, and you tell me!" Nate shot back. "The first few pages are photos of when we were young. The rest are recent."

He yanked open the album and began at the first page. As Nate had said, in the beginning were photos of Mort and Heidi, with their family when the children were little. They looked like a normal, happy family, smiling out at them from the past.

"Beautiful," said Olivia.

"Yeah, it was beautiful for a little while, maybe." Nate's face contorted as he went on.

Nate flipped the pages fast and to Olivia's horror, there were photos of both Penny and Lance filling a couple of pages.

"What are their pictures doing here?" Olivia asked, aghast.

"That's what I asked myself," Nate muttered. "Who are these two? What are they doing in my dad's album? There were no names listed for them, either."

"Didn't you ask your dad?" Olivia managed to ask.

"No, why should I?" said Nate. "I smelled something fishy and I wanted to see what other photos he added to the batch."

Nate began moving the pages forward and before long they were in the present. Olivia now found herself looking at the streets of Nashville.

"Your father took these pictures?" she asked.

"He took some of them," Nate answered harshly, "and I took some, too."

To Olivia's shock, she suddenly saw several photos of Andrea, in at least six different places at obviously different times. Andrea had made it clear that she'd only been in Nashville once or twice.

She'd lied about that! What else had she lied about? Once you found one lie, there was a chink in the armor that couldn't be mended.

Nate turned another page quickly, and there was Andrea again, wearing the exact same necklace Christine had worn that very afternoon!

"How did Andrea get that necklace?" Olivia was jarred. "It belongs to Christine!"

"Christine designed that necklace for her line. She probably has a bunch of them. My father must have given Andrea one of them. Jackass! He was a jackass!"

Olivia was stunned. That was a strange gift to give Andrea. Was Mort secretly taunting both women? Did he enjoy turning one woman against another?

"How did you get this photo, Nate?" Olivia was appalled.

"I told you, I knew something was up, so, towards the end, I followed my father around and took photos of him and the people he was around. This was one of them."

"Was he there when you took this?" asked Olivia.

"Of course he was. How else could I have found her?" Nate looked oddly pleased with himself.

"Your father had no idea you were there, photographing her?" Olivia was incredulous.

"None at all. I know how to hide and blend in." Nate smiled.

"Your father had no idea that you knew Andrea?" Olivia was amazed.

"No, he didn't. He might have been smart but he still was a jackass!"

"That's why you were so annoyed with Andrea when you met her at the station," Olivia suddenly realized.

"Annoyed's putting it mildly." Nate rubbed his hand on the tree stump. "I knew who she was from the get-go."

It certainly seemed as if Mort and Andrea had been having an affair behind the backs of both of his wives. Olivia stared at the brazen photos of Andrea flaunting Mort's wife's jewelry, obviously wanting to take her place. Was this the hard evidence they'd been waiting for?

"Let me see more," asked Olivia, breathlessly.

"You've seen what you need." Nate threw Olivia a strange glance when her phone rang loudly.

"Give me a second, Nate," Olivia said, as she reached over to take the call. "You never know what's happening next. Hello?" said Olivia.

"Olivia, it's Wayne." He sounded urgent.

"I'm with Nate, now," Olivia replied.

"Are you sitting down? There's a new development," Wayne went on hurriedly.

"Oh my God, what?" asked Olivia.

"Christine just got a threatening phone call telling her she's next!" he replied.

"A call from who?" Olivia's head was spinning.

"The caller hung up. We're trying to trace it," said Wayne.

"Oh my," replied Olivia. "When did the call come in?"

"A little while ago." Wayne was agitated. "Angie's totally freaking out. He swears he'll kill anyone who harms his sister. Lance is terrified too. Reporters are blasting the story all over now, asking the public for leads. Between you and me, all eyes are on Andrea, though."

Olivia's mind began racing, thinking of the photos she'd just seen. She couldn't bring herself to say a word about them yet. Too much was happening at once. She wanted to be careful.

"The police want you to go and talk to Andrea again, immediately. You're good with women. They feel safe with you, Olivia," Wayne went on.

"Thanks," Olivia breathed.

"Go and find out whatever else you can about Andrea's relationship with Mort and what she was doing in Nashville, exactly. Who did she see when she went there? See if you think she could have made the call."

"I'm right on it," Olivia replied instantly.

"Good," said Wayne. "I'm teaming up now with Angie and a few cops. We're dead set on tracking down the caller. Once we do, the case will be solved."

"Maybe," Olivia replied softly.

"No maybes about this one!" Wayne was adamant. "The caller threatened Christine's life."

Olivia took a long shot. "It could have been Christine herself for all we know. It would be a wonderful way to take suspicion away from herself and place it somewhere else, wouldn't it?"

"Far-fetched," Wayne replied. "Just get tough with Andrea as soon as you can. My money's on her. And so is everyone else's."

"I'll do my best," Olivia answered, not clear why she just didn't feel Andrea was the killer.

Olivia turned back to Nate swiftly. "I'm sorry Nate. It's an emergency. Someone called and told Christine she was next. I've got to go immediately and talk to Andrea now."

Nate took it in slowly. "Wow," he finally said. "The cops are convinced it's Andrea, aren't they?"

"It doesn't look good for her," Olivia commented.

Nate's eyes narrowed. "Okay, so go. I'll show you the rest of the pictures later."

Olivia felt a great wave of appreciation for Nate. Despite his young years, she felt as though she were with an older person.

"I really appreciate who you are, Nate, and how calm you're being," Olivia remarked.

Nate laughed. "I'm always calm," he replied softly. "If you're not calm how can you see what's right in front of your nose?"

CHAPTER NINETEEN

Olivia arranged to meet Andrea down at the beach immediately, not far from the scene of the crime. By the time Andrea arrived, heavy clouds had set in and the light of day was quickly fading. This was where Mort had often enjoyed walking and where he had been brutally attacked. Olivia wondered if the spot would affect Andrea.

"What's the emergency?" Andrea asked as she rushed over to Olivia.

"Thanks for coming so quickly," Olivia said, suddenly feeling sad for Andrea, who now seemed so forlorn.

"You said there was an emergency, what is it?" Andrea repeated, obviously tied up in knots.

"Christine just got a call from someone threatening her life," Olivia bluntly replied. "The caller warned that she was next."

Andrea lifted her hand to her hair, which the wind was blowing helter-skelter, and smoothed it out rapidly.

"Making a call like that was a stupid thing to do," Andrea remarked. "The police will trace it and bring the idiot in. Then they'll blame the person for Mort's murder."

"It may not be so easy to trace the call," Olivia replied. "Who would do something like that?"

"How would I know?" Andrea looked out over the waves. "Mort loved it down here. He used to come here often."

"Did you come here with him?" Olivia picked right up on it.

"What makes you ask that?" Andrea looked startled.

"Did you come here together often?" Olivia proceeded intensely.

"Who told you that?" Andrea quivered a moment.

"No one," Olivia replied. "I put the pieces together myself."

"What pieces?" Andrea began to grow frightened.

"They were easy to put together," Olivia taunted Andrea, hoping she would unravel and speak the truth.

"I suppose they are easy to put together if you have half a brain in your head." Andrea began breathing heavily.

"You've got to tell me everything you know!" Olivia demanded fiercely. "Did you two come here together often?"

"No, I knew Mort's schedule," Andrea suddenly shot back at her. "When he came here, I would arrive separately. Sometimes I'd slip behind the dune grass and watch him amble along. Other times I'd walk by him on the beach as if we were meeting by coincidence."

Olivia felt chills run up and down her arm. Was Andrea a stalker? Had she driven both Mort and Christine crazy injecting herself into their lives?

"Didn't Mort realize that your meeting wasn't a coincidence?" Olivia became bolder.

"If he did, he didn't say anything about it." Andrea winced.

"You were after him, weren't you?" demanded Olivia.

Andrea laughed. "I wouldn't put it that way, exactly."

"Andrea." Olivia stepped much closer to her, cornering her now. "This isn't a time for hiding. You've got to tell me everything you know," Olivia threatened.

"What makes you think I'm hiding? I came right away to see you, didn't I? Mort's death has hit me harder than anyone else." Andrea's voice had a strange whimpering tone.

"But you're still playing games with me," Olivia dug in.

"I never play games," Andrea retorted as the surf beat more strongly on the sand.

"Yes, you do." Olivia decided to lay everything on the line. "You just said you pretended you just ran into Mort at the beach coincidentally."

"A little white lie." Andrea halted and shrugged.

"And you lied to me other times too, didn't you?" Olivia had Andrea where she wanted her now.

Andrea shivered. "What are you talking about?"

"You told us you were only in Nashville a couple of times at most, right?" Olivia exclaimed.

"Right," Andrea agreed.

"But I saw six pictures of you there," Olivia continued. "Were you stalking Mort in Nashville, too?"

"Pictures of me?" Andrea became alarmed. "What kind of pictures? Who took them?"

"Pictures of you walking around on the streets." Olivia was glad to see Andrea's fear intensify. "In one of them you were even wearing Christine's necklace."

Andrea stopped cold. "Where did you get those pictures?"

"I'm not telling you."

"You have to tell me!" Andrea was now thoroughly alarmed. "Who took those pictures? Where did you get them?"

Olivia refused to answer.

Andrea dug her feet into the sand and stared. "I know who," she breathed finally. "It was Mort's crazy son, Nate! Right?"

"What makes you think that?" Olivia wouldn't let her off the hook.

"Because Nate liked to follow his father around and take all kinds of pictures. Mort complained to me about him plenty of times. Nate thought he was doing it secretly, but Mort knew everything."

"Mort wasn't close to his son?" Olivia was fascinated.

"Mort hated him," Andrea hissed. "He was ashamed of Nate and made no bones about it. That kid is a freak."

Olivia was shocked. "I like Nate," she said.

"Well, you're the only one who does," Andrea spit out. "Nate even has trouble in school. Yes, he's a gifted photographer, I'll grant him that. But ask his teachers. He makes trouble for everyone, and also has a weird gun collection."

Olivia refused to respond to that.

"So, Nate took pictures of me and showed them to you?" Andrea was quickly putting all the pieces together herself.

"It doesn't look good for you, Andrea," Olivia warned.

"This is crazy, it's nuts," Andrea finally yelled out into the early evening. "Nate took all kinds of pictures of everyone and left them everywhere. Mort had a lot of the photos and carried them with him. From time to time I even saw a few of them myself. There were photos all kinds of people. Naturally I wondered who the people were. Then one night in the office I saw Mort sitting there, staring at them. Suddenly it hit me that Mort could have had a whole life somewhere else."

"Did you ask him about it?" Olivia was mesmerized.

"No, I didn't ask him, I told him! I said Mort, I know you have a whole other life." Andrea began trembling violently then. "To my horror he just looked at me and started crying."

"Crying?" Olivia was amazed.

"He sat there crying like a baby and kept saying I'm sorry, I'm sorry," Andrea breathed.

"What was he sorry for? Were you sleeping with him? Was he betraying you, too?" Olivia was aghast.

"No, never! That's not it!" Andrea insisted. "I was not his girlfriend. I just wanted to be his daughter. I wanted him to treat me like he treated the other women in his life."

"So you got him to give you Christine's necklace?"

"It wasn't her necklace, it was one just like hers." Andrea's voice got shaky. "Why shouldn't I have one, too?"

Olivia had Andrea in a corner now, and Andrea knew it. There was no backing out either; things had gone too far. Olivia went back to the heart of the matter.

"What happened after Mort started crying?" Olivia asked.

"Finally, he told me he had another family in Nashville, so that's how I know about Nate," Andrea barely whispered.

"Why would he tell you that?" Olivia was outraged.

"He had to. It was obvious." Andrea suddenly began to smirk. "I knew I had him then. Another family? And he had another daughter as well. Right on the spot I decided it was time for me."

"Now he'd have to give you your just due, wouldn't he?" asked Olivia, horrified.

"What are you talking about?" Andrea's eyes glistened.

"You tell me!" Olivia threatened. "And if you don't, it's all over for you."

"You're right," Andrea breathed. "It was time for Mort to pay up. I decided to blackmail him."

"Blackmail him?" Olivia could have been knocked over with a feather. This was more than she ever expected.

"That's right." Andrea seemed triumphant now. "I told him he'd have to pay up if he wanted me to keep this quiet. When I said that he didn't even look surprised. And pay up, he did. He paid me a hefty check each month so no one would find out."

That had to account for the money that was missing, Olivia realized now.

Now Andrea was on a roll. "He paid up for a long time, but then all of a sudden, the money stopped." She grimaced.

"That didn't feel good, did it?" Olivia zeroed in.

"You can say that again," Andrea hissed.

"So you're the one who called Christine and threatened her life?" asked Olivia.

"No, I didn't threaten Christine at all." Andrea began smiling oddly. "I had no reason to. I did her one better. I went and told Christine about Mort's second family. It was the sweetest conversation I ever had. Maybe Nate made the call, or Calia? After all, they just found out that their father had another wife!"

"Christine knew about Mort's second family?" Olivia couldn't believe what she was hearing.

"Yes, she did." Andrea seemed delighted. "All along she thought that it was only her who was so important, so when I told her, it was wonderful to see her cringe in front of my eyes."

So, Christine had been lying to them, as well! Somehow Olivia wasn't surprised. "What did Christine do after you told her?"

"That was none of my business," Andrea exclaimed. "But believe me, she wasn't the same person again. Penny told me her mother was different, harder to be with. She was upset with Mort all the time. Penny didn't know why, but I did. So, you see, I had no need to make that threatening call. Go find out who did!"

Olivia felt sickened by the story. Clearly, Andrea had no reason for calling Christine. But someone else certainly had. But why? And who?

Then, as wind gusts from the ocean got stronger, Andrea spun around and left, just as quickly as she'd come.

*

Olivia stood alone at the beach and let the breeze wash over her. She could certainly see why Andrea would be the main suspect. But with this new information, Christine was in the woods as well. She'd also lied. If Christine actually knew about Mort's second family, that was also plenty of motive for the crime.

Olivia thought of Nate and the photo album then. What else might be hiding on the pages she'd not yet seen? She decided to return to his hotel room and see if she could look at it.

The wind grew higher and stronger as Olivia stood looking out into the ocean. She wondered what progress Wayne and the police were making tracing the call. Probably not much. If there was more news, Wayne would have let her know immediately. He was good that way, very good.

Olivia paused. Wayne was good in so many ways. He was honest, dedicated, and straightforward. He could also be passionate when he let himself. Olivia missed him and suddenly wished he was here right beside her now.

*

By the time Olivia arrived at Nate's hotel, it was dark out. She went straight upstairs and knocked on the door, fully expecting Nate to be inside.

At first there was no answer. Olivia knocked again, more strongly this time.

In a little while she heard a thin, female voice calling, "I'll be right there. Take it easy."

That had to be Heidi, thought Olivia. Olivia hadn't interviewed her alone yet, maybe this was the time?

122

"What is it? What is it?" The voice came closer as the door opened, and Heidi stood there in a long pale blue velvet robe.

"I hope I didn't disturb you." Olivia took a step back.

"People do usually call before they come to the door." Heidi looked at Olivia, dismayed.

"I'm so sorry," Olivia repeated. "Is Nate here, by any chance?"

"No, he's not." Heidi stood in place without inviting Olivia in. "Haven't you spoke to him enough?"

"We've had some conversations," said Olivia, "and there are just one or two more things I wanted to ask him."

"Well, he's out with his sister having dinner," said Heidi.

Olivia looked past Heidi into the room as if indicating that she'd like to enter. "May I come in for just a little while?" Olivia took the liberty of asking.

Looking almost afraid to say no, Heidi edged to the side, making room for Olivia to walk in.

"Thank you," said Olivia. "I won't stay long."

"What do you want?" Heidi ran her fine hands nervously through her hair.

"I wanted to tell you how sorry I am about your loss," Olivia started, noticing a half full bottle of wine and a glass on the table nearby.

"Thank you." Heidi walked more deeply into the room. "Mort's death is beyond imagination."

"Of course it is," Olivia replied.

"I have no idea how I'll go on without him," Heidi continued. "My life is forever altered. Nothing will ever be the same. I didn't deserve this."

"You'll be okay financially?" Olivia felt concerned.

"Of course." Heidi seemed startled by the question. "Mort provided beautifully for all of us."

"Are you all right down here, now?" Olivia continued, struck by how helpless Heidi seemed to feel.

"Here? You mean in Key Biscayne?" Heidi's eyes fluttered. "It's awful. We're all returning to Nashville in the morning. There's no reason to stay here any longer at all."

"What's awful?" Olivia was interested.

"Everything." Heidi gazed at Olivia strangely.

"You've never been here before?" Olivia repeated the question, just to be sure.

"I told you I hadn't," Heidi said. "Why do you ask again? What difference does it make?"

123

Olivia didn't know why she was asking. She was struck that Heidi and her family were leaving so quickly, before Mort's body had been released.

"I'd have thought you'd wait until arrangements had been made for Mort," Olivia replied.

"Mort will be cremated shortly and we've decided that half his ashes will stay here and half sent up to us in Nashville." Heidi shivered as she spoke. "There's no reason for our family to be here any longer."

"It must be painful to be around Mort's other family," Olivia remarked.

"Painful's not the word for it," said Heidi. "It's disgraceful, that's what it is."

"Heidi." Olivia took a step closer. "You had absolutely no idea about Mort's other family?"

Heidi's eyes flashed wide open. "Any idea that it was real? None!"

"What do you mean real?" Olivia jumped in.

"You know Nate makes up crazy stories. He always has and always will. The past few months he's been telling me crazy things about his dad. But Nate lives in fantasy, so I never believed him."

"What did Nate tell you?"

"I told you, crazy things."

"Like what?" Olivia pressed harder.

"Nate said he thought his father had a whole different life." Heidi could barely get the words out. "I said that's ridiculous, Nate. Your father loves me. Nate said if it's true, prove it, Mom. Prove it."

"What did he mean by that?" asked Olivia.

Heidi suddenly turned into a helpless southern belle and threw her hands up into the air. "How do I know what he meant? I didn't spend my time trying to figure what Nate meant. If I did I would go crazy, just like he is."

"Nate's not crazy." Olivia urgently felt the need to defend him. "I find him inspiring, actually."

Heidi stared at her. "Inspiring? Nate's taken you on a mind trip with him. He does that to people sometimes. Don't let him grab you. Don't believe a word he says."

Was Heidi pointing the finger at her very own son? Olivia was chilled.

"I'm warning you, don't believe him!" Heidi repeated harshly.

But Olivia didn't have to just believe him. She'd seen the photos he'd collected with her very own eyes.

"Okay, it's enough, I have to rest now." Heidi was practically pushing Olivia out the door.

"Thanks for your time." Olivia backed away herself. She wanted to get to her hotel as soon as possible now and talk everything over with Wayne immediately.

CHAPTER TWENTY

Olivia called Wayne from the cab telling him she'd be at the hotel in a little while.

"I'm on my way back now," she spoke quickly into the phone. "I've so much to tell you."

"Great." Wayne sounded delighted to hear from her. "I'll make a reservation for dinner in the little restaurant in the back, overlooking the waterfall."

"Perfect." Olivia was excited. "I'll be there in just a little while."

When the cab pulled up to the hotel, Olivia was eager to get to the restaurant, see Wayne, and debrief. Not only was she hungry, but it always calmed her and gave her a larger perspective when they had a chance to talk.

The way to the restaurant was through the lobby. After she got out of the cab, Olivia quickly walked into the lobby. But as soon as she entered, to her surprise. she suddenly saw Penny rushing toward her.

"Oh my God, I've been sitting here waiting for you." Penny's eyes were red and swollen.

"What happened?" Olivia got scared.

"It's my mom." Penny was beside herself.

Olivia gasped, fearing that Christine had come to harm. "Did the caller get her? Is she safe?"

"Yes, yes." Penny calmed Olivia. "No one has come near her. She's under police protection. There are police officers stationed outside our home. But my mom's definitely become paranoid since that crazy call. It's affected her. She thinks she's next to die and sits at home looking out the window, muttering loudly about my dad. The entire family is freaking out."

"What is she saying?" Olivia felt alarmed.

"It's hard to believe this, but she keeps saying she knew my father had something going on." Penny looked dazed.

Olivia felt a sense of weakness come over her. So, it was true, all true. This turned everything completely around. "Your mother admitted that?"

"My mother says that she told my father that she knew about his second family! And that she couldn't and wouldn't put up with it, either! She warned him there would be hell to pay!"

"When did she tell him that?" Olivia was horrified.

Penny continued uncontrollably. "We had no idea, none of us did. She also said she withdrew money from his private account a few days before he was killed."

Olivia shook her head, as if shaking cobwebs away. She knew this happened at times, that cases unraveled by themselves. Once one thread was pulled, the entire fabric could come undone.

"What should we do about this?" Penny was frantic. "Should we take my mother away and hide her somewhere?"

"Penny," Olivia responded, putting her hand on Penny's arm. "What we have to do is clear as day."

"What?"

"We have to give the police this information," said Olivia.

Penny looked totally shocked. "We can't, we mustn't!" she cried out. "I've hired you to work for us! I'm telling you this in confidence because I don't know what else to do."

"But that's what we have to do," Olivia repeated softly.

"You've got to be crazy! Don't you dare even think that. If you tell them what I've told you, I'll immediately deny every word it!" Penny insisted. "You have no proof. Ultimately, it's your word against mine."

"Do you want someone else to get locked up for something they didn't do?" Olivia looked at Penny squarely.

"Oh my God, my God." Penny started sobbing. "Contact Andrea immediately. She'll know what to do. She always does."

"Why don't you contact her yourself?" asked Olivia.

"I can't, I don't want to! That's why I hired you, isn't it?" Penny seemed frozen with fear. "Just do what I say and call Andrea! Or I'm firing you from the case on the spot. And remember who you're working for. You're not working for the police, you're working for us. And you can be out of here, one, two, three!"

Olivia felt punched in the gut. "We're all working to find the truth, aren't we?" she finally responded.

"You call Andrea and let her tell you what to do!" Penny was growing irate. "And you do what I say. Or before you know it, you'll be back down in Key West with your slippery partner."

"Slippery?" Olivia was stunned. There was absolutely nothing in the world slippery about Wayne. That was the last word anyone would use to describe him. Could be Penny was the one who was becoming paranoid and not her mother?

Penny stormed out then and Olivia stood in the lobby, horrified. Thankfully, in a few moments, her phone buzzed, and she looked down at it nervously.

I'm here in the restaurant. It was Wayne texting. *Where are you?*

I'm in the lobby, Olivia texted back. *Will be there in a second.*

Olivia immediately dashed through the lobby to the restaurant at full throttle.

"What's wrong?" Wayne stood up the second she raced over to the table.

"I've just had a horrible meeting with Penny," Olivia whispered, so glad she and Wayne were finally together.

"Sit down and tell me." Wayne tried to calm her.

Olivia sat down quickly. "Christine's telling everyone that she knew about Mort's second family. She says she fought with him about it and even warned him there would be hell to pay."

Wayne looked startled. "This is incredible news."

Olivia ran her hand through her hair hurriedly, trying to settle down. "I also heard the same thing from Andrea," Olivia continued. "Andrea told me that she found out about Mort a while ago."

"This changes everything," Wayne murmured.

"Not only that"—Olivia's words tripped over one another—"Andrea said that she actually blackmailed Mort to keep the news quiet."

"Wait a minute!" Wayne began to look agitated. "Blackmail is a crime itself."

"Mort paid up for a while," Olivia continued, "and when the checks stopped coming, Andrea got back at him and told Christine."

Wayne was transfixed. "Andrea actually admitted to a crime?"

"Yes, she did," said Olivia.

"Both Andrea and Christine look guilty as hell now," Wayne continued. "We've got to take this to the police."

"I told Penny that," Olivia continued, "and she said we were working for her! We'd be fired immediately if we went to the police. She plans to deny everything she said."

"Did you tell Penny that Andrea corroborated the information?" Wayne's jaw clenched.

"No, I didn't get a chance to," said Olivia. "But Penny wants me to contact Andrea again immediately and find out what to do. She said that Andrea knows that."

"I'm sure she does," said Wayne. "Penny must realize that Andrea's more deeply involved than any of us believed. And just because Christine knew about the second family doesn't mean she

128

actually harmed Mort. If you asked me, the evidence leans more heavily towards Andrea, right now. Hell, she's admitted to blackmail."

"But both of them could deny everything," Olivia went on. "Penny did say that her mother withdrew money from Mort's private account a few days before he died, too. That's on record, at least."

"We can probably trace the blackmail checks Mort paid to Andrea as well, now that we know about them," Wayne added.

"Penny said that she'll fire us if we go to the police," Olivia added.

"That's obstructing an investigation," Wayne said. "Don't let anything they say derail you."

The waiter came over then to take their orders. Olivia's hunger had vanished, though. "I'm not so hungry now," she said when Wayne asked her what she wanted.

"It's okay." Wayne smiled at the waiter. "Bring pasta and salad for both of us anyway."

After the waiter left, Olivia looked at Wayne oddly. He reached out and put his hand over hers. "There's only so far you can go in allowing these cases to upset you," he said in a soft, caring tone. "Dinner is dinner and it's important. It's also important for us to have time alone together."

Despite herself, Olivia smiled. Wayne's barriers seemed to be coming down. And it felt so much better being here with him now. Especially with his hand still on hers.

"I've missed you," Wayne said in a shaky voice.

Olivia was startled and delighted to hear that.

"And the guys on the force have been saying that Justin had taken quite a shine to you, too," Wayne added. "Justin's been talking to them about it. I didn't like hearing that one bit."

Surprised, Olivia smiled broadly. "Jealous?"

"Definitely," Wayne admitted, his eyes sparkling. "And I'm certainly hoping the feeling isn't mutual between you and Justin?" He looked at Olivia searchingly.

"It's not mutual," Olivia answered Wayne slowly. It had to have been hard for Wayne to bring this up and Olivia really appreciated it. "Right now you're the only one I think about, Wayne."

Wayne closed his eyes quickly and smiled as the waiter arrived with a bottle of wine.

"I ordered this for you," he said.

Olivia looked at the wine. "Not right now, though, I don't think."

"No, you're right," said Wayne. "We've got to stay clear and focused for the present. But we can take it back to our rooms for later, can't we?"

What was Wayne suggesting? Olivia wondered

"Of course," she said, lightly, "later, not tonight."

"I'm looking forward to that." Wayne leaned closer to her.

A wave of fear came over Olivia then. It sounded as though Wayne was suggesting that they move forward. The idea was definitely appealing, but she didn't want to be disappointed again.

After dinner, Olivia and Wayne went back to their separate rooms for now, planning to go to the police station first thing in the morning and share the information they'd found. But before he left, Wayne pulled Olivia to him in a warm embrace.

"Once things have calmed down, we'll have that bottle of wine," Wayne whispered to her.

*

Olivia entered her room, her head reeling. So much had happened all at once. She thought of taking a long bath to unwind when her phone suddenly rang. It had to be Wayne, thought Olivia. Did he want to have that bottle of wine tonight? It was too soon, she felt, wondering what she would tell him.

Olivia picked up the phone nervously, and to her total surprise, Nate was on the other end.

"I heard you came to visit my mother," Nate started talking the minute Olivia answered.

"Yes, we had a little visit," said Olivia. "Why?"

"My mother told you we're leaving in the morning, right?" Nate went on quickly.

"Yes, she did."

"I want to see you one more time before we go." Nate's voice got hoarser.

"Do you want me to come to your hotel room again, Nate?" Olivia asked, surprised.

"No, no, definitely no!" Nate seemed alarmed by the idea.

Olivia shivered. "What then?"

"I'll meet you down at the Alaska bar," Nate answered quickly. "I can get in, I have a fake ID. People know where it is, the taxi will find it."

"Okay," said Olivia. She couldn't pass this up and she knew it.

"And don't tell anyone you're meeting me here. Especially my mother!" Nate went on.

"I won't, of course," Olivia whispered, wondering why it was such a secret. "How are you going to get out of your hotel and go, though? Isn't your mother going to ask you?"

"I'm not going for long and Calia will cover for me," Nate responded. "The Alaska isn't far from our hotel, either."

"How's Calia going to cover for you?" Olivia was fascinated.

"She'll tell my mom I'm downstairs in the hotel, having a bite in the restaurant," he said.

"Okay," said Olivia. She didn't want to encourage him to lie to his mother, but also knew this meeting was important. Especially as it was secret. "I'll be at the Alaska in a little while."

CHAPTER TWENTY ONE

The Alaska was a dingy little pub on a narrow side street. No one could possibly even know it was there if they hadn't already heard about it. When Olivia walked in it was crowded, with tinny music playing, smoke, and dim lights. The crowd was mostly younger. Olivia stood there at the bar, looking around, wondering where Nate was.

Olivia suddenly felt a tap on her shoulder and jumped. As she spun around and there was Nate, standing behind her, grinning.

"You got here quick, that's great." Nate seemed excited to see her. "Come to the side of this joint with me."

Olivia followed as he led her through the crowded place to a rickety bench under a shed.

"Where are we?" Olivia asked, looking around.

Nate started laughing. "We're not at Buckingham Palace, that's for sure."

"This is a strange spot," said Olivia.

"That's right." Nate seemed to like that. "And it's the perfect place to talk to you."

"Why?" asked Olivia.

"Stop asking so many questions and let me do the talking," Nate suddenly growled.

Olivia noticed that he was carrying the same large, bulging paper bag. She hoped the photo album was still in it and that he had more pictures to show her.

"We'll go sit in the back where it's quieter," Nate said then, pushing Olivia slightly in that direction.

The two of them made their way to the back of the place, through small aisles between tables and the crowds standing around, talking.

"This sure is a popular place," remarked Olivia.

"It's for the locals," said Nate. "You have to know about it."

"You're not a local though." Olivia turned around and glanced at him. "How did you find out?"

"Calia told me about it," Nate whispered loudly. "Calia knows all kinds of things. The minute she goes somewhere she gets the lay of the land."

"You're close to your sister?"

"Sometimes." Nate smiled.

Finally they came to an empty space way in the back, where the music wasn't as loud and the crowds had thinned out.

"What do you have to tell me?" Olivia turned and looked at Nate square on.

"For starters, I didn't like that you spoke to my mother without me being there," said Nate.

"I didn't know you wouldn't be there," Olivia immediately defended herself. "I actually went back to the hotel room to see you."

Nate smiled strangely. "I thought that," he said, "just checking."

"Why didn't you want me talking to your mother alone?" Olivia couldn't let it pass.

"Because she's a fragile person, and gets unstable," Nate breathed without a pause.

"You didn't want me upsetting her?" asked Olivia.

Nate tossed his head back. "My mom gets upset easily. She spends a lot of time in Nashville in bars, especially when she's unhappy. My dad was gone too much and she was lonely. Don't you dare tell anyone I told you this."

"I won't," said Olivia.

"The people at the bars in Nashville sometimes talk about her. I don't like that, either," Nate continued.

"I'm sure you don't," said Olivia, surprised. "What do you do about it?"

Nate's eyes narrowed. "That's my business," he shot back.

"Did you ever talk to your father about it?" Olivia felt this was important.

"I said it was my business," Nate insisted.

"Okay, okay," Olivia relented. "But you brought me here for a reason, what did you want to tell me?"

"Not tell you, show you." Nate's eyes opened wide then, as he glanced at the big paper bag.

"You brought the album with you?" Olivia was eager to see it.

"That's right." Nate yanked it out of the bag. "We're leaving in the morning, and there's something in here I wanted to you see and fast."

Nate held the album out in front of Olivia. Then he opened it and riffled quickly to a few pages at the end. Olivia held her breath silently, waiting to see what he had to show her.

"Follow me," said Nate, walking a bit to the left, where there was more light.

Olivia followed him to a spot where a bare bulb hung from the ceiling.

"Look at this," said Nate then, holding the album open.

Olivia gazed at the page, where there were several photos of him and Calia. "Very nice," she said.

Nate flipped the page then and there was a photo of Heidi at the beach, under palm trees.

"Recognize this?" Nate asked, his eyes narrowing.

"It's your mother at the beach," said Olivia, not sure what he was after.

"Look where the beach is," Nate urged Olivia forward.

Olivia looked more closely. It certainly looked like the beach was in the Keys. Olivia recognized a lighthouse far in the background that she'd seen on the beach in Key Biscayne.

"Key Biscayne?" Olivia took a long shot.

"That's right! You got it," Nate sneered.

"What do you mean I'm right?" The reality of it hit Olivia. "Your mother said she had never been to Key Biscayne!"

"She did say that, didn't she?" Nate started grinning.

"What are you telling me, Nate?" asked Olivia. She wanted to hear from him exactly what he was thinking.

"I'm telling you that my mother lied," Nate said between clenched teeth.

Olivia looked at the photo more closely. "Your mother lied about where she was?"

"Definitely," Nate agreed.

"Can I have this photo?" Olivia asked then. The police could check it out, she imagined.

"No, you cannot." Nate drew the album away.

"We need solid evidence," Olivia pressed him.

"But you can't have it," Nate repeated. "You know where she was and you'll always know it, but there's nothing you can do about it, either."

"Nate, this is crazy." Olivia reached for the album abruptly.

He pulled it further away harshly, spun around, and ran out of the place.

Olivia stood there looking after him, rattled. She wondered if what Heidi had said was true. Was Nate living in a strange fantasy world? Or did he have real information that he couldn't bear to tell the world?

Confused, Olivia quickly put a call in to Wayne. She knew he'd be sleeping by now. But she had to talk to him anyway.

"What is it? What's going on?" Wayne mumbled, half awake, when he picked up the phone.

"I'm sorry to wake you up, Wayne," Olivia started.

In a second he was more alert. "What happened? Where are you? I'm coming down to your room."

"I'm not in my room," Olivia said quickly.

"Where are you?" Wayne sounded frightened.

"I'm down at a dingy little place called the Alaska," said Olivia. "Nate called after we spoke and told me to meet him there immediately. He and his family are leaving first thing tomorrow morning. So I had to go."

"Not alone! You should have taken me with you," Wayne insisted.

"I had no choice."

"It's not smart to go to strange places alone at night. That's what I'm here for."

"Nate's a kid and I know him. We've talked before. He's shown me the photos in that album he keeps with him."

"Okay, so what did he want?"

"He showed me a photo of his mother, Heidi, on a beach that he said was down in Key Biscayne."

"So?" Wayne seemed unimpressed by the news.

"Heidi told us she'd never been in Key Biscayne," Olivia insisted.

"So, are you sure that's where the beach is?" asked Wayne.

"Not positive," Olivia admitted.

"Her crazy son could have even take the picture when she was here this time, couldn't he?" Wayne continued.

"It's possible, but doubtful," Olivia said.

"This is a detour and a distraction." Wayne was wide awake now. "Nate's probably shocked that his father is gone and developing all kinds of fantasies. Maybe he even thinks it could be his mother. People always blame someone else in the family. It doesn't add up to anything."

"I don't agree," Olivia said softly.

"Listen," Wayne continued. "The police are bringing Christine in for further questioning first thing in the morning. I gave them the information we have, and they're all over it. They're also going to grill Andrea again shortly."

Olivia swallowed hard. "We're going to get kicked off the case, Wayne," she finally said. "Penny will realize we told the cops."

"Let her realize what she wants," said Wayne. "The truth is the truth and we're going to get it. Come back to the hotel now and get to sleep right away. We have to be at the station first thing in the morning to hear what Christine has to say."

*

Olivia got back to her hotel room quickly, but couldn't sleep. The photo of Heidi on the
beach bothered her. It bothered Olivia even more that Nate would show it to her. Was he just
trying to create confusion? Was he framing his mother and possibly covering for someone else?

Whatever Nate's motive, it was unsettling. Heidi and Nate certainly had a strange relationship. Olivia was sorry that they were returning to Nashville so soon. She even wondered if the police could restrain them and keep them here just a little bit longer. It might be too late to do that now, but they could certainly bring them down here again for further questioning. Olivia hoped that might happen, as she finally closed her eyes and drifted off to sleep.

CHAPTER TWENTY TWO

Right after breakfast, the next day, Olivia and Wayne made their way to the police station in eager anticipation. It was cooler than usual today with a light rain that tapped lightly on the roof of the cab.

"This could be it," Wayne said in the cab as they sat close to each other. "If Christine is really unraveling, we could be on the brink of a confession from her."

Olivia shivered. "If she's unraveling how reliable is her confession?"

Wayne smiled. "You're sharp, Olivia. Nothing escapes you. You're right, of course, but that's how most confessions are made. The person doesn't see any way out and can't keep the truth locked up any longer."

"And if it's a false confession made out of desperation?" asked Olivia.

"Some are," Wayne agreed, "and it's up to us to figure it out. People's lives are on the line."

"And it's up to us to protect them," Olivia quipped. It all seemed like a huge burden to her suddenly.

"Don't worry." Wayne seemed to pick up her feeling as he put his arm around her and gave her a light hug. "You're not alone with it. None of us are, ever."

When they got into the police station, Christine was there already, running her hand frantically through her hair and shifting back and forth restlessly on the bench she was sitting on. Chief of Police Dowl and a few other officers were there, including Justin.

"I can't take another minute of this," Christine burst out as Olivia and Wayne entered and sat down.

"Just repeat what you told us one more time." Dowl was leading the interrogation.

"Why do I have to repeat it again? Why didn't you hear what I said the first time?" Christine stared at him bitterly.

"We heard it." Dowl stayed professional with her. "We need to hear every word of it again to be positive."

"I told you I hated the bastard and I'll say it again now," she suddenly burst out. "Mort and I were having a terrible time before he died."

"That's not what you said before," Dowl corrected her.

Christine raised her eyes to the ceiling. "I said that I knew he had a second family for a while now, is that what you're waiting to hear?"

"Exactly," said Dowl as the other officers in the room looked at one another.

"I knew it, I knew it." Christine's voice rose as she repeated the words. "And I had a right to hate him, didn't I?" She threw an off-glance at Olivia then. "Didn't I? Tell them, Olivia."

"A person has a right to feel whatever they feel," Olivia responded. "It's what they do about their feelings that matters."

"What did I do?" Christine half rose from her seat, "I yelled at him, I told him I knew about his second family. I begged him to tell me why. Wasn't I enough for him? Didn't I give him my life?"

"What did he say?" Olivia was spellbound.

"He denied it completely, every word of it," breathed Christine. "I told him that Andrea told me and he said she was a troubled young woman. Why would I believe her instead of him?"

"Mort played with your head," said Olivia.

"I actually think he believed every word he said," Christine muttered. "He probably never thought of them as a second family. He must have thought of her as the whore she was!"

"What about their children?" Olivia urged her on.

"She trapped him, I'm sure of it." Christine looked devastated. "I warned him there would be hell to pay for getting involved with that kind of woman! There always is. What would you do, Olivia?"

Christine's question took Olivia aback. "I don't know," said Olivia truthfully, as she looked over and saw Justin gazing at her.

"You'd want to kill the bastard, too, wouldn't you? Anyone would." Christine's face was flushing.

"I might have that feeling," Olivia continued, "but I wouldn't do it."

Christine laughed.

"Did you kill him, Christine?" Olivia asked forthrightly.

The question obviously took Christine by surprise. "Of course I didn't kill him."

A deep silence suddenly swept through the police station.

Olivia stood up and walked closer to Christine. "But you just said you wanted to."

"It wasn't only the second family either," Christine went on, her rage intensifying. "I begged him over and over to get Andrea out of our lives. I couldn't stand her. And he wouldn't! He could have, but he didn't."

"How could he have gotten Andrea out of your life?" asked Olivia.

"He could have told her to get the hell out of our home," Christine thundered.

"Wasn't Andrea your daughter's best friend?" Olivia plunged forward. "Didn't she come over to see Penny?"

"Andrea's a miserable creature who was after my husband." Christine was emphatic. "She wouldn't leave us alone. She stalked us."

"You felt she wanted to take Mort from you?" Olivia wanted to be precise and clear.

"Andrea wanted everything I had," Christine breathed. "She'd give us the sob story that she had no father, but she didn't want a father. She wanted my life."

Dowl took a few steps closer to Olivia and Christine. "Andrea should have been here half an hour ago," he said.

"Good." Christine looked half wild. "When she comes in she can tell you how she blackmailed Mort and when he didn't pay up, she came and told me what was going on. She's a poisonous snake in the grass."

"Where is she?" Wayne asked Dowl then.

"Damned if I know." Dowl was disconcerted. "They're looking for her right now as we talk."

"She's probably out somewhere killing someone else!" Christine shouted.

"Or maybe someone's got her?" Justin joined in now, looking at Christine oddly.

"Got Andrea? I'm the one they called warning, not Andrea." Christine went on the attack. "I'm the one to be worried about, not her!"

"And maybe you're after her now, defending yourself?" Justin was vigorous and held nothing back.

Christine stopped and stared at him strangely. "You're young and you're smart," she hissed. "Maybe I am?"

"Maybe it's you who wants Andrea dead?" Justin moved closer.

"Of course I do." Christine flared up uncontrollably. "Why shouldn't I? Wouldn't you?"

Dowl put his hand on Justin's shoulder to pull him back. Justin shrugged him off and moved closer.

"There's a lot of people you want dead, aren't there, Christine?" Justin moved in for the kill.

"I do, I do." Christine started shouting. "Get the hell away from me, you little monster, or I'll get you too!"

Justin threw a quick look at Dowl then. Dowl nodded harshly.

"We're going to have to hold you here, Mrs. Townsend," Dowl suddenly said.

"Hold me, why?"

"Under suspicion of murder," Dowl replied.

"You just try it," she blasted.

"We have to," Justin responded matter-of-factly. "You're a danger to yourself and others."

*

"That's it," Dowl said as Christine was taken from the room. "We've got what we need."

"Definitely looks like it," agreed Justin.

"Not so quick." Wayne took him on abruptly. "We can't discount Andrea. Where is she? Why didn't she show up? We've got to take her in anyway as she clearly confessed to blackmailing."

Justin shrugged. "Big deal," he quipped. "Christine is obviously the killer. She hated her husband. She found out about his second family and confessed to wanting to kill him."

"He denied it though," Olivia jumped in. "And Christine believed him."

"She believed that he wasn't actually married to Heidi, but there's no denying he cheated on her for a long time."

"We need hard evidence, though." Wayne spoke to Justin as if he were a newcomer.

Justin didn't like it. "I'd say this is as hard evidence as you can get."

"Hold on, hold on." Dowl got between them. "Both of you are right. Christine is loaded with motive, but we can't discount Andrea. It's not good that she didn't show up, either. If we don't locate her in a little while we'll put an all points alert out on her."

The idea of that frightened Olivia. "If Andrea's on the run, an all points alert could push her over the edge," she said. "I think it's best to search for her quietly."

Justin smiled at Olivia warmly. "We might not have the luxury of that," he said. "Right now time is of the essence."

"Olivia is right," said Wayne, bristling and wanting to put a wedge between her and Justin. "If Andrea sees we've got an all points alert out, it might drive her into real hiding."

"Let's calm this down for a minute." Dowl jumped in again. "All likelihood, Andrea will show up any minute. The good part is that right now we have two definite persons of interest, Christine and Andrea. From here on in, we've got to focus all our attention on both of these women. For all intents and purposes, outside of them the case is closed."

Closed? Olivia was dismayed. "Not yet," Olivia insisted.

Wayne looked at her carefully. "They're not saying it's totally closed," he reminded her, "just that we know where to focus now."

Everyone in the room was then given assignments about what to look into. All eyes would check out every aspect of both these women. There would be a definite conclusion, they felt, in no time.

*

Olivia and Wayne headed back to the hotel for lunch before embarking upon their individual

assignments. Olivia was to talk to all of Andrea's friends and acquaintances, in the effort to find out more about her life and background. Did she have a secret record that no one knew about? Wayne was teaming up with a few other officers to dig more fully into Christine's marriage, family, and finances.

"Justin's an impulsive, brash kid," Wayne commented as the cab pulled away. "And not that bright, if you ask me."

Olivia smiled. She knew Wayne was threatened by Justin and she liked that.

"He's okay," Olivia said blandly. "I've seen better and I've seen worse."

"Who's better?" asked Wayne.

"I'll give you three guesses, Wayne," Olivia remarked.

"You're talking about me?" asked Wayne, laughing.

"Yes I am," Olivia reassured him. "Who else?"

*

When Olivia and Wayne arrived back at the hotel, Olivia felt tired. She wanted to go up to her room to freshen up a little and said she'd meet Wayne at the coffee shop in a few minutes. Naturally, Wayne agreed. Olivia also needed time alone to go over everything. She decided to take a quick shower, change, and try calling Andrea

141

on her own. Olivia was concerned about her. Perhaps she'd get an answer and find out where she was easily.

The shower felt warm and wonderful, washing the tiredness away. Olivia stood under the pouring water, realizing how uneasy she felt about the case. There were too many loose threads dangling to be anywhere near declaring it closed.

When she got out of the shower, Olivia slipped into a lovely lemon silk, summer dress and brushed her hair for a long time. Her grief over Todd's death was fading and Olivia felt the time was coming to move forward in her love life again. Her closeness to Wayne was definitely growing and it was fun that Wayne felt jealous of Justin, but what did it mean actually? Although they worked so beautifully together, Olivia realized that she didn't know Wayne personally so well. Who was he as a man? What was important to him? So far their work as detectives had consumed both of them. It was definitely time for both to open up and learn more about each other.

Just as Olivia was about to go down to meet Wayne in the coffee shop for lunch, her phone suddenly rang, stopping her.

CHAPTER TWENTY THREE

"Hello?" said Olivia, picking up her phone quickly, hoping that Andrea might be on the other end.

But to her surprise it was Nate calling.

"Olivia, Olivia," Nate spoke hurriedly, "I just heard the news."

"What news?" asked Olivia, confused.

"We're back in Nashville now and got a call from the police," Nate went on. "I heard they think Christine's most likely the killer."

Olivia was horrified. "Why would the police tell you that?"

"My mother begged them to keep her updated." Nate's voice got lower. "One of the cops on the force took a liking to her. He feels badly for her and said he would."

"Which one?" asked Olivia, startled.

"I don't know his name." Nate became rattled.

"Was it Justin?" asked Olivia.

"I told you I don't know," said Nate.

"Well, okay, thanks for letting me know that," said Olivia.

"That's not all." Nate seemed scared that Olivia was about to hang up. "Listen to me!"

"I'm listening," said Olivia, agitated by the call.

"Christine didn't do it. I know that for a fact," Nate went on.

"How do you know that for a fact?" Olivia was riveted. "Give me the details."

"Just listen to me and don't ask any questions." Nate was insistent. "You've got to come up to Nashville immediately. I'll give you an address to visit. Go there as soon as you arrive. You won't be sorry."

"Nate, please, talk to me straight," Olivia pleaded. "Whose address is it?"

"I am talking straight. I couldn't be straighter." Nate breathed heavily. "And come fast. That stupid Andrea is down here now, bugging my mother."

"Andrea's at your home?" Olivia was amazed.

"You said it." Nate didn't like it one bit. "She keeps telling my mom that she never had a father, and Mort was the father she always wanted."

Olivia was appalled. Now Andrea was stalking Mort's other family. "What does Andrea want from your mother? Money?"

"I'm not sure," said Nate quickly, "but whatever she wants, she's not going to get it. I'll see to that."

Olivia began trembling. Was Andrea totally insane or was she a master manipulator, and possibly a killer? Was she hiding out in Nashville now?

"I'm texting you the address I want you to go to," Nate went on. "After you go there, you can come to our house and deal with Andrea yourself."

"Okay, I'll be there shortly," Olivia swiftly replied.

"You will?" Nate sounded overjoyed.

"Yes, definitely," said Olivia. "If Andrea's down there, I have no choice about it."

"And even if she wasn't," Nate went on, "you've got to go to the address I send you first."

"You won't tell me who lives there?" Olivia asked one more time.

"I can't," said Nate. "You'll find out yourself soon enough. Just get up here as fast as possible."

Olivia hung up the phone, agitated. What was Andrea really doing in Nashville now? For

all they knew she was the one who'd made the threatening call to Christine. Did she now have designs on Heidi as well? It certainly seemed possible.

Olivia couldn't wait to get downstairs to talk to Wayne about this. She walked to the door quickly, when suddenly her phone rang again.

"Yes, what is it?" Olivia answered, disconcerted.

"Olivia, this is Calia," a shaky voice sounded on the other end of the phone.

"How are you, Calia?" asked Olivia, strangely relieved to be hearing from her. "And how is your family? Are all safe and well?"

"Safe, yes, definitely. But are they well? That I don't know," Calia responded. "My brother just told me that he was going to call you. Did he?"

Olivia became silent. "Why do you ask?" she replied.

"Please, whatever Nate says, don't believe a word of it," Calia went on in a hurried tone. "He's totally cracking up and dreaming up wild scenarios. And he's trying to pull everyone in. This happens to him from time to time. He's freaking out now because my father died and is blaming everybody."

"He sounded fine to me when I talked to him." Olivia felt driven to defend him.

"Nate's not fine though, and he never was," Calia insisted.

"Is there anything else you have to tell me?" Olivia asked then. "Something you might be leaving out?" Olivia wondered why Calia was really calling.

"Leaving out? Nothing." Calia sounded offended.

"Is Andrea there with you, too?" Olivia had to know more instantly.

"Yes, what of it?" Calia replied casually.

"What's she doing there, Calia?" Olivia's sense of urgency intensified.

"Nothing much," Calia replied. "Andrea's sad and says she came down here to comfort me. She'd love to have me as a second sister."

"You can't be that to her!" Olivia was appalled.

"Why not? What's so bad about it?" asked Calia.

"Be careful," Olivia breathed. "Andrea's behavior is not normal."

Calia laughed. "It's my brother who's not normal," she insisted, "and I'm calling to warn you about that. Tell me what he told you over the phone."

Olivia instantly decided not to say a thing about her conversation with Nate to Calia. Olivia would go to Nashville immediately and talk to everyone there herself.

"I'm coming to Nashville in a little while," Olivia said to Calia. "Make sure Andrea stays there with you. I need to talk to her, too."

*

When Olivia finally got to the coffee shop, Wayne was on his third cup of coffee.

"You took such a long time," he commented as she quickly slipped into the booth.

"I'm so sorry, Wayne," Olivia replied. "I got two unexpected calls I had to answer."

"From who?" Wayne was interested.

"First from Nate and then his sister, Calia."

"Interesting," Wayne agreed. "Nice that they stay in touch with you."

"More than interesting, a bit alarming," Olivia went on. "First Nate said he was positive that Christine did not commit the murder."

Wayne raised his eyebrows skeptically. "Positive?"

"Then he told me he wanted to give me an address in Nashville that I had to visit immediately," Olivia continued.

145

"Whose address?" Wayne didn't like that.

"He wouldn't say who," Olivia answered, "but he said I wouldn't be sorry."

"There's no end to the amateur detectives floating around," Wayne replied. "When they don't give you specifics, it's meaningless. It's some kind of game they're playing."

"There's more than that," Olivia spoke over him. "Nate said that Andrea was with his family in Nashville right now."

That definitely stopped Wayne cold. "Andrea's in Nashville? You're sure?"

"Yes, and then Calia called right after and corroborated it." Olivia declined mentioning to Wayne what Calia had said about Nate.

"What's Andrea doing with the family in Nashville?" Wayne didn't like it.

"Calia said Andrea told her that she'd love to have Calia for a second sister," breathed Olivia.

"That is weird." Wayne shuddered.

"More than weird," said Olivia. "Andrea's definitely pathological."

"Looks like it," said Wayne conclusively.

"I'm going to Nashville as soon as possible," Olivia continued, "both to visit the address Nate gave me, and to talk to Andrea."

Nate shook his head slowly. "Wrong move, not necessary," he remarked. "We can get the police to bring Andrea back down here. There's no need to track her in person."

"I also want to visit the address Nate gave me," Olivia repeated.

"That doesn't make any sense at all." Wayne wouldn't go along. "And you can't do it alone anyway."

"I can call the Nashville police for backup," said Olivia.

"Absolutely not," Wayne objected. "What's the point of it? Why won't Nate tell you whose address it is? You can't go running around following all kinds of false leads and fantasies. This is a time for focus."

"How do you know it's a false lead?" Olivia objected. "Nate led me right to Andrea, didn't he?"

"If she's really there," Wayne grumbled. "Let's call her and see."

Olivia didn't want to do that. "No, I want to catch her there unaware."

"It won't work. I can't go with you now." Wayne's voice grew deeper. "We're all zeroing in together here on what's at hand."

"Well, my assignment was to find more about Andrea." Olivia was adamant. "So, this fit right in."

"Your assignment is to talk to all kinds of people and acquaintances in Andrea's life," said Wayne. "You need to get undercover, secret information, not talk to her again."

"Who knows what else is in Nashville, waiting to be discovered?" Olivia wouldn't budge now.

"Olivia, when a case comes to a boil it's very common for all kinds of false leads to come out of the woodwork," Wayne declared. "I've seen this happen time and again."

"Finding Andrea is not a distraction," Olivia retorted.

"If you really find her, even," said Wayne.

"Nate's wired in, he knows something." Olivia had to defend him again. "Someone on the police force even told him that they feel Christine is the culprit."

"Who did that?" Wayne was shocked.

"Nate didn't remember their name," said Olivia.

"How convenient," remarked Wayne. "This guy is slick, he covers up everything. The cop he talked to probably was Justin, anyway."

"I asked him that," said Olivia. "He said he didn't know who."

Wayne finally shook his head hard. "This is all nonsense and distraction. Let's stay right here and keep to our plan. It's great that you found Andrea, if you did. I'd like to check it and then have her brought back immediately."

"No," said Olivia in a firm voice. "My gut tells me to get on the next plane and catch her in person."

"Please, Olivia, don't do it," begged Wayne.

"It's a short trip. I'll be back in no time. And I'll give you the address of the place I'm going to check out," she replied.

Nate reached for what was left in his cup of coffee. "Do what you have to," he said then, irritated. "Obviously, there's only so much impact I can have once you've made up your mind."

"I have no choice, I have to follow my heart," Olivia replied. "I'm nothing without that."

"I know, I get it," Wayne said as he drained his coffee cup dry.

*

Olivia rushed back upstairs to pack for her trip and make reservations on the first plane to Nashville. To her dismay, Wayne went back to the police station after their lunch, to resume his assignment. He said the guys were waiting for him. Olivia was on her own. It was good to be on her own, but also she wished that Wayne would have been more supportive. He seemed to go back and forth, very warm one moment and totally professional the next.

Once the plane was booked, Olivia texted Wayne all the information, including the address to visit that Nate had sent her.

Thanks for this, Wayne's text quickly arrived. *Keep me informed of what's happening.*

Olivia was upset. His text couldn't have been more distant. Wayne was probably upset that she was taking things into her own hands, and going to Nashville despite Wayne's objections. But this wasn't a matter of making him feel good. Too much was at stake. A life had been lost and for all they knew others were in danger. Olivia had to do what she felt was right. She could never live with herself, otherwise.

The cab drove to the airport quickly and Olivia arrived in plenty of time. As she sat in the passenger section waiting to board, a feeling of great loneliness came over her. It would have been nice if at the very least Wayne had accompanied her to the flight. Everyone around seemed to have someone with them.

Finally, the announcement came that her flight was boarding. Olivia took her carry-on bag and got in line. As she walked through the gate and gave them her pass, for some reason she turned around for a second. To her surprise, there was Wayne, rushing in toward the plane, waving and calling.

"Olivia, Olivia, have a safe, easy trip," he called as he came closer and closer.

Olivia lifted her hand and waved back briefly, as the boarding line moved forward and she was pushed into the plane, out of sight. Olivia longed to turn around and run out to greet him, to wait for the next flight together. Had he come to go with her, or just say good-bye? The fact that he was there meant a great deal to her. Even though he'd arrived a moment too late.

CHAPTER TWENTY FOUR

Oddly, the plane was half empty even during early evening, when it was usually full. The flight went smoothly, however, and Olivia arrived in Nashville in no time at all. As she walked through the crowded airport, Olivia couldn't help think of the time Todd died. As now, she'd felt totally alone and unanchored. Even then, in those awful moments, she knew it would be up to her to help find Todd's killer. That knowledge had disturbed her then. She'd tried to shake it away and dismiss it. But by now she realized that it could not be dismissed. Olivia had no idea why she'd been chosen for this mission, but by now it did feel like a mission. She knew she was traveling along a path that was inevitable and had belonged to her from the start. But, along with a sense of isolation at times, there was also the feeling that Olivia was doing what she was here to do, living her life to the fullest. That feeling bolstered and strengthened her deeply.

As always, Olivia first checked into the hotel she'd be staying at, before she made her first stop.

Her hotel was small, but charming and lively, overlooking a beautiful garden. Once in her room, Olivia thought about contacting Wayne and letting him know she'd arrived. She didn't really want to, though.

True, he'd come to the airport to see her off, but still, she felt odd about it. Olivia also thought about contacting Nate or Calia and telling them she arrived. Once again, she decided not to. She wasn't truly sure what either of them were going through, and it was always better to arrive unannounced, before they had a chance to prepare.

Once settled in and changed, Olivia decided that the first stop would be to the address that Nate had given her. She'd have more clarity, for sure, once that was explored.

Olivia went downstairs immediately and took a cab through winding streets of Nashville, which were bustling with life, out onto a highway which seemed to be leading to a suburb on the edge of town.

"I don't get too many calls to go here," the taxi driver commented as they drove along.

"Why not?" asked Olivia.

"It's out of the way, a dead end," he responded. "Nothing much happens here, especially

during the evening."

Interesting, thought Olivia, as the cab wound off the highway through slim streets that seemed somewhat deserted, leading nowhere. A few large homes were placed way back, along these streets, but mostly big, old trees stood in the forefront.

"Who lives around here?" Olivia asked the cab driver.

"Darned if I know," he replied. "People with money, I guess. Maybe old-timers who like quiet? Maybe they get off on seeing a leaf fall from a tree. Nothing much else really going on."

Olivia wondered exactly where the driver was taking her, and who would be there when she arrived.

In a few moments he turned into a long, narrow cul de sac. "The address you gave me is at the very end of this street," he announced.

The cul de sac seemed especially deserted, with no lights on in the homes. Olivia thought of

asking the driver to wait for her. It might be hard to get someone to take her back.

"Can you wait for me?" she suddenly asked.

"For how long?" He seemed surprised.

"Not long, maybe half an hour at the most," Olivia replied. "I'll pay for your waiting time."

"Where do I take you to then?"

"Just back to the hotel you picked me up at," she said.

"Sure thing," he said then, turning around to look at her closely. "It's not going to be cheap, though."

Nothing is cheap, thought Olivia. There's a price to pay for everything.

"It's okay," she said. "I could be back sooner than half an hour."

Olivia stepped out of the cab then, in front of what looked like an empty mansion, with a large stucco porch in front. The furniture on the porch was old and beside a few birds perched on the railing, no lights were on, and no one seemed to be around.

Olivia walked along the long entranceway to the front door and stood in front of it thinking that Wayne might have been completely right. Nate could have sent her on a wild goose chase, based on his fears and fantasies.

Olivia quickly pulled out her phone and texted Wayne. *I'm here at the address Nate gave me.*

She stood on the porch and waited a while for an answer. To her dismay, none came. Okay, she finally decided. Time to knock on the door and see what happens then.

Olivia lifted the large, old-fashioned knocker and hit it loudly on the old wood.

Some crickets in the background chirped loudly, as if answering her. Olivia lifted the knocker and tried once again.

Again, no answer. This had to be some kind of hoax, she decided then, about to turn around, when suddenly she heard a female voice calling from inside.

"What do you want? Who is it?" The voice sounded familiar.

"It's Olivia Wells," Olivia called back strongly.

"Olivia Wells?" The voice grew fainter.

Olivia lifted the knocker and banged more harshly. "Open up! Let me in!"

The door flew open then and to Olivia's shock, Heidi stood there in a flowing, blue robe.

"Heidi?" Olivia was dumbstruck.

"What in the world are you doing here?" Heidi was equally dumbstruck.

"Can I come in?" Olivia finally managed to say.

"No, you cannot. How did you find this place?" Heidi was shaken to the core.

"Please let me come in," Olivia pleaded. "I've come from far."

"I don't care," Heidi stood her ground.

The two women stood there staring at each other. Suddenly Olivia saw someone appear in the background. His was big, handsome, brawny, and young. As he came closer, Olivia saw a huge tattoo on his forearm.

"Get back, Charles." Heidi began quivering.

"Let me in, Charles," Olivia called out over Heidi's voice.

"Who the hell is this?" Charles pushed Heidi back and stood in front of her, confronting Olivia.

"I'm a friend of the family," Olivia couldn't help but remark.

"She's a detective!" Heidi's voice rose loudly.

Charles's lip curled as he stared at Olivia. "How'd you get this address?" he demanded.

Olivia knew she could not tell him. "I heard about it," she offered lamely.

"From who?" Charles wasn't playing any kind of game.

"Tell her to go home, please," Heidi was now trembling. "Tell her to turn the corner and leave us alone."

To Olivia's surprise, Heidi's pleas seem to have an effect upon Charles.

"It's okay, sweetheart, I'm taking charge," he murmured to her.

Taking charge of what? Olivia wondered. Heidi's life and resources?

"Let me in," Olivia said again boldly, not entirely sure why she wanted to enter so badly.

"Anyone with you?" Charles looked around carefully.

"Only a cab driver waiting at the edge of the road to take me home," Olivia said.

Charles smiled strangely, suddenly looking Olivia over carefully. "You're young and you're beautiful," he said then. "What the hell are you doing here alone?"

"I need to speak to both of you." Olivia didn't flinch.

"First tell me who gave you the address and then I'll let you in," Charles replied.

"Nate gave me the address," Olivia decided to say.

"I knew it, I knew it," Heidi gasped.

"Don't worry." Charles turned to her forcefully. "I told you I'm taking care of everything. And I am, I will."

"You're not taking care of Nate though." Heidi's eyes rolled upward.

"I'm taking care of whatever needs to be taken care of," Charles insisted.

"Oh my God, my God, not Nate." Heidi was screaming by now. "My own son, turning on me."

"Come in," Charles said. "Olivia is here to help us, Heidi." He turned to her. "She'll let us know who else is on to us and what the hell they want."

Onto them? Olivia looked at both of them closely as Charles pulled the door wide open and yanked her in.

It was dark inside and musty, with bare wooden floors. Olivia walked with them into a sitting room that was messy, with clothing strewn around and smelled like stale wine. In the back of the room a door was open, leading out to the big yard.

As soon as they walked in Heidi quickly ran around, picking up stray pieces of clothing from the floor. Obviously Olivia had barged into their secret love nest.

"Who lives here?" Olivia asked again now.

"What's it to you?" Charles grew tougher.

"What are you doing here?" Olivia wasn't backing down.

Charles laughed suddenly. "Honey, if that isn't obvious, then nothing is."

Heidi stepped forward bravely, pushing Charles to the side. "Charles is my lover," she announced suddenly as if thousands were here to receive the news.

Olivia was at a loss as to how to respond. "I'm sorry to hear that," she said finally.

That was the wrong response, though. "Oh really?" Heidi's voice got louder then. "Why shouldn't he be? Mort left me alone all the time, year after year."

"Mort was with you half the week," replied Olivia.

"What's half the week?" Heidi's eyes flashed in the small light that was on in the corner.

"So, you've had a lover all these years?" Olivia exclaimed.

"No, I haven't," Heidi stepped forward shrilly. "I was loyal, too loyal and everyone knows it."

"Then she met me." Charles grinned proudly.

"It wasn't that I just met him." Heidi was on a roll.

"It was that you found out about Mort's second family?" Olivia finished her sentence.

"Right! How did you know?" Heidi was startled.

"Because I saw the photo of you in Key Biscayne, even though you told us you were never there." Olivia tried to unnerve her.

"Saw the photo?" It took Heidi awhile to take that in. "How did you see it?"

"Nate must have showed it to her," Charles burst in. "Your lousy kid is after you, sweetheart, and you'd better face the truth."

"Is it true, did Nate show it to you?" Heidi began trembling.

"I saw it," was all the Olivia could say.

"You saw it and what?" Charles wanted more information.

"I saw it and realized that you were in Key Biscayne for a reason," Olivia filled in.

"Yes, I was, and it was a very good reason." Heidi calmed down. "Andrea contacted me and asked me to come down. She said she had something important to tell me."

"Something important to tell you for a price!" Charles reminded her.

"That's right, for a price," Heidi conceded.

So Andrea was making money on Mort's trouble any way she could, Olivia realized.

"Andrea told you about Mort's second family when you came down?" Olivia asked.

"That's right, exactly!" said Heidi. "She even showed me pictures of them to prove it."

"It all cost a pretty penny, too," Charles thundered.

"Everything isn't money, money, money, Charles," Heidi insisted. "I found out the truth and it shook my world. Everything started spinning. That's when I met Charles. I had a right to be with him completely. If Mort had two wives I thought, why couldn't I have such one young, handsome lover?"

Charles smiled proudly then.

"How long ago did this start?" Olivia asked.

"When I got the news from Andrea." Heidi began to whimper. "And I've never been happier, either, if you want the truth. Our love has grown deeper and deeper. We found this place to be together in and moved in. We can't stand to be apart for a second, can we Charles?"

Charles spun around, a dark look on his face then. "No, we can't," he repeated, suddenly glaring at Olivia. "It's a shame you came down here to visit, the whole thing is a shame because you're nice, I actually like you. In fact you seem like a terrific person to me."

"Shut the hell up," Heidi railed at him now.

"You seem like the kind of woman who could hold the world up," Charles continued. "It would have been different if we met in other circumstances." His dark eyes narrowed.

"What are you talking about?" Olivia managed to ask then, as Heidi drew closer.

"What do you mean if you'd met her in different circumstances?" Heidi glared at him furiously.

Without another word, Charles lunged forward and grabbed Olivia's shoulders hard.

"I'm so sorry, but we can't let you live now that you know about this!" he growled. "We can't let you go free? How can we?"

Olivia's entire body began trembling as she tried to push him away. She couldn't. Instead, his hands began to circle around her neck.

"Get it over with fast," Heidi called out to him. "Get rid of her fast! Fast! I can't stand her."

"Get rid of me?" Olivia gasped for air. "Just like you got rid of Mort?"

Charles laughed. "You got it, honey, and it will go fast. It'll just take a second. Your neck will snap like a twig in the wind."

Not my neck, thought Olivia, outraged as she lunged away from Charles for a quick second.

"Tell me what happened first," she managed to beg. "What difference will it make? Nobody will know."

Charles laughed hoarsely. "Sure we'll tell you, why the hell not? It'll be fun to tell you. Tell her, Heidi."

Agitated, Heidi began pacing back and forth. "I don't want to," she breathed.

"You have to," he insisted. "It gives me pleasure to hear about it again."

Suddenly Heidi stopped pacing, came close to Olivia, and stared. "It wasn't enough for Charles and me, living in hiding like this." Her voice grew piercing and shrill. "I couldn't stand it and I told that to him. We have to do something, Charles, I begged him. I love you, we have to be together all the time."

Olivia felt terrified. "What did you have to do? Come out into the open? Divorce Mort?"

"There was no way I could divorce Mort," Heidi suddenly whimpered. "Charles and I both needed his money. It's my money too. I deserve it. I've been married to him all these years. There was a nest egg he'd saved just for the two of us for when we got older. He always showed the balance in that bank account to me. That was my money, sitting there, just waiting for me. There was no other way to get free, none at all." Heidi lunged toward Olivia. "But the rest was Charles's idea."

"To kill Mort?" Olivia gasped.

"It wasn't my idea." Charles waved her off. "Every night Heidi fed the idea to me. We've got to get him out of the picture, Charles, she kept begging. Then we've got to get rid of the other wife, too."

Olivia felt a long chill rise through her body. "You're the one who made the threatening call to Christine?" she breathed.

"That's right." Charles threw his head back. "I wanted the other wife to know what was coming up ahead. That way she'd be more jittery, and slip up. She'd look over her shoulder wherever she went and make big mistakes. That's how it happens."

"Heidi sent you down to Key Biscayne to take out Mort first though, didn't she?" Olivia glared at him. The pieces all suddenly fit together. "You two killed Mort in cold blood."

"That's right, Heidi sent me down." Charles grinned. "It's a shame you asked me so bluntly. I got there right before the storm and waited for the bastard. We knew he'd be there because that's what he did, walked in that spot at the beach during all kinds of weather. The idiot enjoyed storms, enjoyed trouble. The minute I saw him I rushed up to him from behind, grabbed him, and put my hands around his neck. He gave one shout, tried to twist around to see me, but it was over in a second. I threw him down onto a big rock, standing there, and he died the minute his head hit it. It was too quick, too easy. Then I had my fun, bashing his face in."

"Your fun?" Olivia was breathless.

"You never said it was fun before," whimpered Heidi.

"We all have our fun in our own ways, don't we, honey?" Charles pulled Olivia a little closer to him.

"You're both monsters," Olivia breathed, furiously.

"Oh, really?" Charles sneered as his hands started closing around her neck.

Outraged, Olivia suddenly rallied. She decided to use her last burst of energy to swing sideways into Heidi and with her full strength, knock her down.

Olivia lunged to the side and crashed her body into Heidi's. Stunned and off balance, Heidi fell to the floor with a sudden shriek. The next sound Olivia heard was Heidi's head knocking on the wooden floor. Then her painful moaning.

"What the hell did you do? What the hell happened?" Charles was beside himself as he swiftly let go of Olivia and swooped down to Heidi's side. "Heidi, Heidi, open your eyes. Talk to me."

In that moment Olivia gasped for air and, trembling, fled out the open back door into the backyard. Once outside she dove into the tall bushes in the yard, hiding. Her heart was pounding. She was here, she was alive. She crouched down for dear life and drank in the cool evening air. Outside it was silent. Charles did not come out after her. Olivia had no idea what was going on inside.

First thing she had to call Wayne, and then she'd find a path to the driver waiting for her at the end of the driveway.

Wayne picked up the instant his phone rang.

"I'm in the back of the house, hiding," Olivia whispered.

"Hiding?" At first Wayne seemed uncomprehending. "Don't move. Stay where you are. I'm not far away. I'll have local police get there instantly."

"Not far away?" Olivia was confused.

"I took the next flight after yours." Wayne breathed hard now. "I couldn't let you do this alone."

"Heidi was at the address Nate gave me with her lover. Heidi's lover tried to kill me, the way they killed Mort. They did it together." Olivia could barely speak. "I had my recorder on with me. It's over. We've got them."

"My God," breathed Wayne, "you were right again! How could I have been so stupid? Please, please forgive me!"

CHAPTER TWENTY FIVE

It seemed like no time at all before Olivia saw a swarm of police spreading out over the back of the house. What had happened to Heidi inside? Olivia kept wondering, as she stayed crouched and motionless inside a tall bush. Charles had not come out either, looking for Olivia. He was either frightened of being discovered or probably assumed Olivia was gone after all this time. Of course that didn't mean he wouldn't be after her shortly. Olivia knew too much now to be safe.

As one of the policemen came close to her hiding place, Olivia stuck out her arm to reach out for him.

"Oh my! Okay," he muttered under his breath. "Don't move. I've got your back."

The policeman slowly took Olivia's arm and pulled her out of the bramble, beside him. Her dressed was torn, her face scratched, and Olivia felt as though she would faint.

"Your partner's on the way," the policeman whispered to her. "The other cops are going into the house now."

Olivia cringed, not knowing what they would find. Was Heidi still alive? Was Charles there with her? Or had he killed Heidi too, to wipe out the evidence?

"I heard you're a heroine," the policeman said to her excitedly. "Congratulations."

But Olivia couldn't make sense of what he was saying. Instead, at that moment, she saw someone running toward her from the side of the house. To Olivia's deep relief, it was Wayne.

"Olivia," Wayne called out, pulling her to him. "You're okay?"

"I'm fine," she whispered.

"I'm sorry, so sorry." Wayne's words tripped all over one another. "I realized what an idiot I was when you boarded the plane and I immediately took the next one. You mean so much to me, too much! That's why I've been such a fool. It won't happen again, though, I promise. Forgive me, please."

"I'm so glad you're here," Olivia whispered, putting her head down on his shoulder.

"Glad isn't the word for it," Wayne answered, as he held her closer, then gently picked up her face and once again drew Olivia into a long, powerful kiss.

Police soon circled the house, creating a dragnet before a few officers decided to venture inside.

Dead silence surrounded the area, as everyone waited to see what they would find.

To everyone's relief, in a few minutes the police emerged with Heidi and Charles, alive and well. A flurry of activity took place then as both Heidi and Charles were immediately tossed into a police car, which swiftly took off down the road.

"They're both alive, they can walk!" Wayne was ecstatic. "Case solved."

"I thought they'd both be dead," said Olivia, "that they'd kill each other off."

"Don't worry, they're as good as dead now, with the evidence you've got," Wayne murmured.

"I have a cab waiting for me down at the end of the road," Olivia said. "Let's go to it."

Olivia felt a bit wobbly as she started to walk. Wayne propped her up as they headed to the cab, which was still waiting for Olivia down at the end of the road.

"What's going on?" The driver turned to greet Olivia.

"Thanks so much for waiting," she whispered.

"Sure thing," he replied. "Something told me there as going to be trouble as soon as you left the cab. I mean, I immediately thought, what the world is a young woman like her doing in a place like this? Then, later the police poured in."

Olivia and Wayne got into the car and the driver pulled away then, turning on the radio.

"Case of man murdered in Key Biscayne solved," came blaring over the news.

"Solved? Solved?" the driver exclaimed. "Is that what happened here? You solved the case?"

"The news is out already." Olivia turned to Wayne.

"Once again, the bravery of Olivia Wells has turned a tragedy into a victory," the reporter went on fervently.

Olivia and Wayne smiled at one another as they drew closer together. "I'm so proud of you," he whispered. "Thank God you didn't listen to me!"

Olivia smiled. "I listen a lot of the time and I value your input. This time I just couldn't."

"And you were right, one hundred percent right. Not only that, to celebrate we're leaving for a vacation immediately after everything has settled down," Wayne added. "We'll go anywhere you like. You need it, I need it."

The idea sounded wonderful to Olivia. She couldn't think of anything better than being away alone with Wayne. "Can't wait," she said, snuggling closer to him.

"And we're going even if other calls come in for cases," Wayne added. "And they will, I guarantee you. The phone lines in our office are probably ringing off the hook now that the news has come out. But remember, this time, it's us first."

"Agreed," said Olivia as they drew together in a long embrace, and as Wayne had predicted, her phone started ringing.

"Don't pick it up," Wayne warned. "Some will be calling with congratulations and some will be desperate to hire both of us for a case that's just waiting to be solved."

*

There was one stop that had to be made, though, before Olivia and Wayne could depart. The next day both families gathered in the police station in Nashville. It was odd to see them all together now. The sense of both shock and relief in the room was palpable.

Calia and Nate, looking devastated, sat on the side close to one another. Penny and Lance were standing beside both of them, offering comfort. On the other side of the room, Angie had his arm around Christine, and Andrea sat by herself at the end of the table, tapping her fingers on it solemnly. She looked dazed, forlorn, and frightened. Chief of Police Andy Pern was also there, to oversee the meeting.

The moment Olivia and Wayne entered, everyone stood up in appreciation.

"I know I speak for everyone here when I offer incredible thanks to both Olivia and Wayne," he started.

"Yes, yes, thank you, thank you," everyone said all together.

"I was just waiting for you to get here," Pern added, "before I make a few announcements."

All eyes turned to Pern in anticipation.

"This has definitely been a rough road for everyone here," Pern started. "Not only does the police force wish to formally acknowledge and thank Olivia and Wayne, I'm sure the families do as well. We're in awe of the bravery displayed by Olivia and the outcome of the case. This was the last thing anyone expected."

"Thank you, thank you, thank you," those in the room repeated again.

"Right now, the case is officially over," Pern continued. "Heidi and Charles are in custody without bail."

Everyone gasped. It was shocking to hear that so conclusively. The case was over; what happened next?

Pern then turned to Andrea. "And," he continued, "the information Andrea contributed was essential to solving the case. Therefore, we've received the request that any other possible charges be dropped."

Andrea's head dropped down when Pern said that. Olivia knew Pern was referring to possible blackmail charges against Andrea. She wondered who had requested that they be dropped.

"This request was made by Mrs. Christine Townsend," Pern went on.

Andrea's eyes shot open and she stared at Christine. "Really? Really? Thank you," she murmured.

"Thank you," Christine responded back to her.

Christine's response surprised Olivia tremendously. It seemed like her ordeal had changed her. Was it possible that something positive could come out of this nightmare?

"Naturally, we are concerned about the well-being of both Calia and Nate," Pern continued then.

"I'll see to it that they're cared for," Lance spoke up boldly, the new head of the family now. "If Calia and Nate wish they can come to live in Key Biscayne and my sister and I will look after them."

Calia's head dropped into her hands as she started sobbing. "I do want to come, I do," she murmured. "And Nate will come with me, too."

Lance put his arms around both of them then. "I'll do my very best for you, I promise," he said.

Christine and Angie got up then and walked over to Olivia. "You did a wonderful job, both of you," Christine said as she threw her arms around Olivia. "We'll never forget this."

Penny ran over and joined them, close to tears. "We lost a father but now we have two new siblings. Who knew?"

Olivia felt overwhelmed. This was why she did what she did. There was no better reward than moments like these. Wayne, too, was deeply touched.

"Nothing in the world makes us happier," he replied, "than to be part of the healing."

"What's next? What are you doing next?" Lance came over and joined Wayne and Olivia.

"Well, for starters, Olivia and I are taking a little vacation alone," Wayne announced proudly.

"Good for you," said Penny, smiling. "You've definitely earned it."

Wayne smiled. "Yes, we have and it's definitely time," he responded.

But Pern swiftly interrupted. "Well, maybe it's time and maybe not," he said. "Right now we have at least three urgent calls for Olivia and Wayne."

"Oh no," breathed Olivia as everyone shuddered.

But she wouldn't be taking any of them.

At least not now.

About Jaden Skye

#1 bestselling author Jaden Skye is author of the bestselling romantic suspense series CARIBBEAN MURDER, which includes 16 books (and counting), and which begins with DEATH BY HONEYMOON (Book #1).

Jaden is also author of the romance series A PERFECT STRANGER.

Jaden is also author of the new romantic suspense series MURDER IN THE KEYS, which begins with NO PLACE TO DIE (Book #1).

Jaden has always been fascinated with mystery, wrongful death, lies, deception and the power of the truth to prevail. Her romantic suspense/mystery novels feature strong female protagonists who must overcome insurmountable obstacles, and through them, she seeks to get to the very heart of the nature of justice and love. Please visit www.jadenskye.com to find links to stay in touch with Jaden via Facebook, Twitter, Goodreads, her blog, and a whole bunch of other places. Jaden loves to hear from you, so don't be shy and check back often!

Books by Jaden Skye

THE CARIBBEAN MURDER SERIES
DEATH BY HONEYMOON (Book #1)
DEATH BY DIVORCE (Book #2)
DEATH BY MARRIAGE (Book #3)
DEATH BY DESIRE (Book #4)
DEATH BY DECEIT (Book #5)
DEATH BY JEALOUSY (Book #6)
DEATH BY PROPOSAL (Book #7)
DEATH BY OBSESSION (Book #8)
DEATH BY DEVOTION (Book #9)
DEATH BY BETRAYAL (Book #10)
DEATH BY REQUEST (Book #11)
DEATH BY ENGAGEMENT (Book #12)
DEATH BY SEDUCTION (Book #13)
DEATH BY TEMPTATION (Book #14)
DEATH BY INVITATION (Book #15)
DEATH BY WEDDING (Book #16)

THE TOM'S RIVER SAGA
A PERFECT STRANGER (Book #1)

MURDER IN THE KEYS
NO PLACE TO DIE (Book #1)
NO PLACE TO VANISH (Book #2)
NO PLACE FOR VENGEANCE (Book #3)
NO PLACE FOR MARRIAGE (Book #4)
NO PLACE TO DECEIVE (Book #5)

THE KILLING GAME
INVITATION TO DIE (Book #1)
INVITATION TO MADNESS (Book #2)
INVITATION TO AGONY (Book #3)

71463795R00093

Made in the USA
Middletown, DE
24 April 2018